JOURNEY OF PASSION

To Dawn
I hope you enjoy
Ralph McCaulsen

JOURNEY OF PASSION

BY

ROBERT M. HAWKINS

Copyright © 2000 by ROBERT M. HAWKINS

All rights reserved.
No part of this book may be reproduced, stored in a retrieval system, or transmitted by any means, electronic, mechanical, photocopying, recording, or otherwise, without written permission from the author.

ISBN: 1-58721-892-5

1stBooks – rev. 7/17/00

About the Book

This is an emotional, tender and sometimes funny story about ranch life, a strong relationship between father and son, and a beautiful woman who melds into their lifestyle.

ONE

She stirred slightly emerging from a deep sleep, but her painful movements brought her to consciousness. She lay still a few moments while unfamiliar sounds echoed in her ears. Listening intently to the intermittent fluttering sounds, she opened her eyes to a faint light. Could it be early dawn, or the twilight of evening? She didn't know. "Got to get up...got to get up," she said, pushing herself upward on her hands, but the effort was tiring and she slumped back.

Not knowing where she might be, she struggled to her feet. Her movement caused a flurry of commotion, and she saw a flock of sparrows vacate the nearby bush.

With her eyes wide and her mouth agape, the sight of her surroundings dispelled her pain momentarily. "Where am I? Dear God, what's happened?" Her mind raced frantically, but no answers came. She clutched the brush to keep her balance, then steadied herself at the base of a large pine tree.

Dazed and bewildered, she leaned against the tree. The pain returned to her body. She had no recollection why she was here, or what had happened to put her here. She looked down at her feet, realizing one shoe was missing and the heel of the other one torn off.

Her head throbbed and her body ached. She raised her hand to her head, then instinctively jerked it away from the painful touch. The sudden movement caused her head to spin, and a nausea filled her. She stood motionless until the feeling passed, then gingerly felt the spot on her head again. Her hair was stiff with matted blood. The sleeves of her blouse were torn, exposing deep scratches on her arms. The calves of her legs had fared no better.

Once more her mind called out for some answer, but there was none, and she felt the sense of shock setting in. She mumbled to herself, taking stock of her condition to calm her mind.

"Take it easy. I'm going to be all right. I have no broken bones. It's warm, so I won't freeze. All I have to do is walk, and I'll eventually see someone who can help."

Wiping her eyes dry with the back of her hand, she looked upward. Above her, she spotted a steep, rock covered slope. To her left, the tree's bows bent to the murmuring breeze, playing a mournful tune. Below her, about two hundred feet, lay thick brush and more large pine trees. The small draw bottomed out, then gradually rose on the other side.

Soon the natural instinct for survival took over, and she started to pick her way down the slope. She struggled through the buck brush, occasionally finding an open spot where the going was easier. Confused, in pain, and with no sense of direction, she climbed to the top of the ridge. She saw nothing from her vantage point except the gentle rolling hills of meadowland, dotted by a tree here and there.

"Oh, God...how did I get here?" She asked herself over and over.

The temperature started rising. Beads of sweat trickled across her head, and dirt smeared her face when she wiped her eyes. Her auburn hair was a tangled, knotted mess, and her dress clung uncomfortably to her moist body.

For two days she wandered aimlessly, stumbling, and occasionally falling. But each time, she stubbornly picked herself up and continued on...and on. At night she lay huddled under a tree, terrified of the strange night sounds and the horrifying darkness, hoping and praying for the sun to rise quickly.

The relentless sun had awakened her. Wet with sweat she picked herself up. It was the third day, her throat and tongue were dry. Her lips were split and her eyes mere slits. Fighting to keep her balance on weary legs, she fell to the ground. Her spirit struggled once more to regain her feet, but she lacked the strength. She knew she was dying. What had brought her to this place of hell? Her numbed mind searched for the answer, but her memory was blank, and she slipped into unconsciousness.

Her senses were aroused when she felt a cool moisture caressing her face and cracked lips. A trickle of liquid penetrated her parted lips. Slowly, her eyes opened, and, through blurred vision, a face appeared before her. Again she felt the coolness applied to her face and neck, then more of the life-giving liquid spilled over her lips and down her throat.

Her eyes tried to focus on the face, but all she could make out was hair, scraggly hair, the hair of an animal. She struggled to get away.

"There now, miss. Everything's going to be okay," a voice said in gentle tones.

Her eyes focused. She saw that it was a man, bracing her body against his. He raised the canteen of water to her mouth.

She grabbed at the canteen, but he pulled it away. "Take it easy, not too much at once."

She licked at her cracked lips, feeling the roughness against her tongue. She gazed into the blue eyes of the bearded man, and managed a, "Thank you."

"Lady, you're sure a lucky one...lucky I came by. What the heck are you doing out here?"

"I...don't know. Where am I? Who are you?"

"Not much wonder you can't remember. That's a nasty cut on your head. My name's Malloy, Bob Malloy. What's yours?"

She looked at him blankly, while searching her mind for a name. But nothing came to her. She turned her face away, embarrassed at not being able to remember just that one important detail, her own name.

"Well, no matter," he said. "We got to get you some medical attention. Think you can ride?"

Her eyes never wavered and she remained silent. He leaned her against the tree, then withdrew his hunting knife.

Her eyes opened wide, and she screamed, "Oh God, help me...help me." She backed away fast.

"Hold on...hold on, I'm not going to hurt you." He had the knife in front of her and split the dress up the middle.

"Can't ride a horse in that tight thing," he said.

His eyes dropped momentarily, and the dress fell away, exposing her thighs. They were scratched and bruised. It had been some time since he'd seen so much of a woman's legs, especially such well-shaped legs. He looked past the scratches and the bruises. His eyes lingered for a moment and he felt an urgency in his loins.

His gaze traveled upwards into lovely eyes of emerald green. He stared at her for a moment, absorbed by concern for the condition she was in. "Come on, we better get you to the doc's."

He helped her to her feet, then picked her up in his arms. They approached his horse, and the animal nickered at the sight of them.

"Whoa, boy," he said.

After hoisting her into the saddle, he climbed aboard behind her and pointed the horse in the direction of his ranch.

They rode in silence. Bob couldn't help but wonder why she had been wandering so far from the main road. Though her hair matted with dried blood, her clothes torn, and her arms and legs scratched and bruised, he detected a certain sophistication about her.

He asked again, "What's your name? I got to call you something."

She remained silent for a moment. "I...I don't know," she sobbed, her voice cracking. "I can't remember who I am. What's wrong with me?"

Bob thought she was going to faint, so he tightened his grip around her. "Just hold on, miss. I'll get you to the doctor, and he'll fix you up. Try to stay calm; it's not much further to my ranch."

They crossed a meadow of plush, tall grass, then dropped into a draw. Following it for half a mile, they angled upward to the ridge of the slope. They started down, and spotted what she presumed was his ranch. The rambler-style house sat nestled behind a line of poplar trees. To the left of the house, a distance of one hundred yards, sat a big barn, corrals and several smaller out-buildings.

"Is that where we're going?"

"Yep, that's home."

When they hit the flat approaching the house, a young boy ran out to meet them. He wore a tee shirt stuffed into his jeans and boots that overlapped his pants. The pants were too big and the belt that he wore was tight. He was tall for the age of twelve. His red hair, a tangled mess, glistened in the sunlight. He held his hand to block the sun out of his eyes. "Gosh, Dad, who's that?" he asked, seeing the woman.

"Lady got herself hurt, boy. Got to get her to Doc Woodward right away," he said, stepping off the horse, then helping her down.

"Is she hurt bad?" the boy asked.

"Don't know, for sure. Here, son, put this horse up and feed him. I'll be back soon as I can."

"What about Old Blue?"

"Can't worry about him now," he replied, leading her to a pickup truck parked near the house.

"Is that your boy?" she asked, watching him lead the horse to the barn.

"Yep, name's Stephan," Malloy answered, opening the door for her. He helped her into the pickup, knowing she was in pain, so he wasted no time in getting her to Doctor Woodward's.

Winthrop, Washington, a small town with an old western atmosphere, sported false-front buildings and planked boardwalks that played to the drugstore cowboy. The novice, who enjoyed the flavor of the old west, could exercise his fantasies over a weekend, some merely dressing the part, while others, more adventurous, participated in horse and cattle ranch operations.

When they reached the doctor's office, Bob helped her to the door. The outside resembled the western look of the town, but the inside was modern. He walked her to the counter and the receptionist greeted them.

"Hi, Bob." Mable's eyes opened wide, seeing the condition of the woman, and immediately came to her side.

"This lady's had some sort of accident, and she needs looked at pretty quick."

The receptionist saw the swollen, blood-matted area on the side of her head and said, "I'll take her right in."

Bob started for the door. "Thank you, Mable. I'm going down to the marshall's office and tell him about her."

She turned her attention to the woman and led her into an examination room. Mable was tall and light skinned, and had a long drawn face. She wore a pinkish white uniform and old worn tennis shoes. She reached for the blood pressure machine on the wall. "My Lord, what happened to you?"

The woman put her arm out to accept the blood pressure machine. She desperately tried to remember, but there was nothing. She eventually said, "I don't remember."

"Well, it's reading 140 over 80. The doctor will be in shortly."

In five minutes the doctor walked in. His eyes first caught sight of her bloodied head, then quickly scanned the rest of her.

He helped her to a prone position on the examining table, then worked in silence trimming the hair around the wound. Sponging warm water over the gash, he washed away the last of the dried blood by blotting it with a cloth.

"The wound to your head isn't bad," he finally said.

"It sure hurts, though, Doctor," she moaned, sitting up.

"I'm sure it does, and probably will for a few days. How did this happen?"

The woman looked directly at him, her attention focusing on him for the first time. He was tall and slim. The aroma of his shaving lotion diminished the medically clean odor of the room. His white coat was unbuttoned, and she took note that he wore a blue western-cut shirt, casual slacks, and shiny boots. A large silver belt buckle, embossed with a horse's head, adorned his midriff. His gray eyes bore into hers, silently, waiting for an answer.

"I...I...don't know. I just found myself in this strange place in the middle of nowhere. I don't know how I got there."

She felt his large, ham-like hands on her head, and wondered how his touch could be so gentle for such a large man.

"I'll dress that head wound now," he continued. "Fortunately it won't need any stitches. Many head wounds of this type could cause a temporary memory lapse."

"Doctor, can you tell me just where I am?"

"Yep, you're in the state of Washington, and this little town here is called Winthrop."

"That's where?" she exclaimed.

"West, yep, unless you go to Seattle," he said.

She stared straight ahead, asking herself, `How did I get here?'

Bob informed the marshall about the woman, where he'd found her, and that he'd taken her to Doctor Woodward's office. Since the marshall wanted to interview her, Bob decided to kill some time in Three Fingered Jack's, one of the local saloons.

While he sat drinking his beer, the mysterious woman consumed his thoughts. Through the dirt, sweat, chapped lips and tangled hair, he could see that she was an attractive woman. He wondered who she was, and where she had come from. Oh well, he thought, it was none of his business. Doc Woodward would take care of her. After all, he'd done what he could to help her.

He left the saloon and got into his pickup, then headed out of town. He passed the doctor's office, and he felt a compelling need to see if she was all right. He parked the vehicle and sauntered into the office. Mable was at the counter assisting a patient with insurance papers. When the patient left, Bob approached her.

"How's she doing, Mable?"

"I'm sure she'll be okay. Come with me," she said, beckoning.

She opened the door leading to the back rooms, and he followed her to her work station. She sat down and said, "The marshall just left. I think the doctor must still be with her. It's good you stopped in, Doctor Woodward wants to see you. He should be out soon."

"What's he want with me? I just thought I'd check and see how the woman is doing."

Just then, Doctor Woodward emerged from one of the patient examining rooms and approached Bob.

He stood up and took his hat off and laid it on the seat. His six-foot frame carried a new white western shirt with the sleeves partially rolled. His jeans and boots had seen better days. He wore no belt and the jeans fit snugly around his waist. His black wavy hair didn't meet with the shaggy beard that he wore. His forehead was strong, setting off his blue eyes.

"How's she doing, Doc?"

"She has a loss of memory...temporary, I hope," the doctor said.

"Yeah, but I can't figure how she got here, or what happened to her. It looked to me like she'd been wandering around for days. So what are you going to do?" Bob asked.

The doctor shrugged his shoulders. "There's not much I can do. I'll keep her here a couple of days to make sure she's gonna' be okay, but beyond that, I don't know. The poor woman has no identification. She can't tell us who she is, not now. I'm sure somebody will be lookin' for her, sooner or later. How did you happen to find her, anyway?"

"I found her on Big Craggy Ridge. Old Blue jumped the damn corral last night, and I'd been looking for him since daybreak. It just happened that I saw her laying there in plain sight."

"It's a good thing you found her as quick as you did. She could have been out there for some time and ended up in real bad shape. That bruise on her head will be tender for a while, but there's no concussion. She'll probably have a headache for a day or so, but I gave her some pain killers to help ease that."

"Well, I got to be getting back to the ranch," Bob said, stooping to pick up his hat and moving toward the door.

"Just a minute, Bob. I was just thinkin'...you know it might be a good idea if she stayed with you and Stephan out at the ranch."

Bob's eyes opened wide and his jaw dropped. He looked at Doctor Woodward and Mable. He had dark feelings. "Stay with me! She can't do that!"

"Why not? It would just be for a few days," the doctor continued. "I'm sure someone will show up to claim her. In the meantime, she may even get her memory back."

An uneasy feeling came over Bob, and he started fidgeting with his hat. "Oh, I don't know, Doc..." he said, shaking his head negatively.

"There ain't a room to be had in town. Like I say, I want to observe her a couple of days and that means havin' someone stay with her. Now Mable has agreed to stay here with her, but she needs a place afterwards that's a little more comfortable."

The doctor could see the frown on Bob's face. His lips were drawn tight, and the eyes pleading...no.

"Look, Bob, so far, you're the only one she knows, or is at least familiar to her. Right now, she's frightened, confused, and needs help."

He stood for a moment, mulling the idea over in his mind. "Ah...I don't know, Doc. I'd like to help her, but I don't think she's the type of woman who would enjoy staying with us. When you dig past all the dirt, she looks like one of them citified women."

"Hmmm..then you sensed it, too," the doctor said, smiling. "There's something about her, and it makes me curious. Besides, I'd like to know the reason for her bein' up there lost in the hills."

"Maybe she'll get her memory back in a couple of days. You said it was temporary, and then--"

Doctor Woodward was quick to interrupt, "And maybe it'll take longer than that, hell, we can ship her out to a hospital in Seattle or Spokane, but she's got no money. Right now, as I see it, it's up to us to help her."

"Yeah, well...since Laura's gone, it's just been the two of us. I'm not sure how Stephan would cotton to a strange woman in the house."

"It's none of my business, but I think it would be good for Stephan to have a woman around. I know how he feels after loosin' his mother, but that's been three years ago. The boy has to get over it some day. Sometimes I don't know if you're givin' in to his whims or protectin' yourself."

Surprise flashed in Bob's eyes at the doctor's charge. "What the hell's that supposed to mean, Doc?"

Doctor Woodward looked at him sharply. "Now don't go gettin' your tail feathers ruffled. That's somethin' you have to figure out for yourself."

Bob felt the pressure Doctor Woodward was putting on him. He also felt sorry for the woman, but she wasn't his responsibility. Then he envisioned her in a lonely room, cooped up by herself, not being able to remember anything, not even her own name. He thought of how he would feel in that position.

"How long do you figure before she'll get her memory back, or someone comes looking for her?"

"I'm sure it would only be for a few days. And, you would be doin' her a good turn."

Bob nervously shifted his weight from one foot to the other, and he again fidgeted with his hat. He searched his mind for any excuse for not having her stay at the ranch. His gaze shifted between the Doctor and Mable. "Seems to me she should have a woman looking after her. Isn't there somebody else who could take her...Mable maybe?"

"I would be happy to have her stay with me, but my place is just a one bedroom apartment," Mable replied.

"But it isn't right...a strange woman living with us. People will get the wrong idea."

"To hell with what people think," the doctor scoffed. "Damn it, Bob, the ranch is a quiet, peaceful place for the girl to heal up."

Bob gaped wistfully at Doctor Woodward and Mable, and they stared back in silence.

"Well, all right, I'll try it," he finally said reluctantly. "But only as a favor to you, Doc."

"Good, I'm sure you won't regret it. I'll tell her you'll be pickin' her up in a couple of days." The two shook hands and then Bob left.

Mable stood behind the doctor. "You're a sly one, Doc," she said.

Doctor Woodward turned to face her. "Well, someone's got to get him to move off center," he said, "And it might straighten out Stephan in the process."

"And you might be interfering where you shouldn't be," Mable interjected.

"Interferin'!" Doc exclaimed, then jerked his thumb toward the back room. "That girl's in serious trouble unless she gets her memory back. The ranch is a much better place for her than being cooped up in this town."

"You know very well what I mean, and don't try to camouflage your intentions. You've already given yourself away. I'm talking about somebody we all know. You know she's had her eye on Bob."

He met her steady gaze, then winked. "I know," he said, grinning slyly. "I want you to go pick somethin' up for the woman to wear. You know, underclothes, a dress of some sort, shoes, and maybe a sleepin' gown. Have 'em bill it to me. While your doin' that, I have one more chore to do."

"What's that?"

"Well, now I got to convince her the ranch is the best place for her."

"You mean, you haven't talked to her about it?"

"Nope, but I'm fixin' to if you'll get out of here and do what I told you to."

The woman lay quietly on the hospital bed. Doctor Woodward approached her, and she looked up at him, her eyes questioning.

"How are you feelin'?" he asked, and he drew a chair up to the bed.

"A little better, except for my head. What's the marshall going to do? Can he help me?"

"I'm sure he'll do all he can. I suppose the first thing is to fingerprint you and see if that produces your identity."

"How long will that take, Doctor?"

"I'm not sure...probably no more than a few days. I don't want you to worry now. We're goin' to take good care of you. I sent my nurse to get you some new clothes to wear."

"That's very kind of you, but I have no money," she said, then started to sob softly. "What am I going to do...I-"

"Now, now, I don't want you worryin' about that. The important thing is to get you on the mend. Right now I'm your doctor, and I want you to follow my prescription."She gazed into his soft eyes. "What kind of prescription, Doctor?"

TWO

When Bob Malloy returned to Doctor Woodward's office, he was tense, but his anxiety was more concerned with his son Stephan, than the woman. It had just been the two of them for the past three years, and Stephan opposed any threat to the image of his mother. In fact, Bob didn't even mention he was coming to town to bring the woman back.

"She's in the next room; I'll tell her you're here," Doctor Woodward said.

She walked into the waiting room, carrying a brown paper bag containing the few clothes Mable had purchased for her. Her face was etched with apprehension. She looked at Bob, she then glanced at the doctor and Mable, then back to Bob. "The doctor has suggested I spend a few days at your ranch to rest. I hope it's not an inconvenience."

Bob shot a quick glance at Doctor Woodward. "No, ma'am, if it'll help get your memory back. But I can't be calling you, hey you...you got to have a name. What would you like us to call you?"

She couldn't help but notice the stiffness in his voice. This was going to be an awkward situation, she thought to herself. "I don't know; anything, I guess. It's only going to be temporary anyway."

"Why not make it Jan?" Mable suggested.

"Fine, I like that," she said.

"Well, Jan, shall we head for the ranch?" Bob asked, opening the clinic door for her. On the way out, he tossed a glum look at the doctor, then quickly closed the door.

Jan climbed into the pickup with Bob's assistance. She could sense the tension in the air. While they rode in silence for several miles, she would steal quick glances at him. With his hat tilted back on his head, she could see black wavy hair. She guessed his age to be around thirty-five, but with that mound of hair on his face it was difficult for her to tell. "You really didn't want to do this, did you?" she finally asked.

He didn't answer her; just kept his eyes glued to the road. The hardened, disgruntled attitude he exhibited was enough for her to know that this was not what he wanted. She noticed he wasn't wearing a wedding ring, but he had a son, which meant he must have a wife.

"Look, Mister Malloy, I really appreciate everything you've done for me, but I don't want to cause any trouble between you and your wife. Why don't you just take me back to Doctor Woodward's? I can take care of myself." She tried to sound pleasant and grateful, but it was rather difficult with the attitude this man was showing.

"Don't have a wife. I promised Doc you could stay with me and the boy for a spell. Leastways until somebody comes for you."

Once again, they rode in silence. Jan turned her eyes toward the side window, searching her mind desperately to remember something of the past, but everything was a complete blank except for the events of the recent days. What was she going to do? Tears began trickling down her face. Not wanting him to see, she quickly wiped them away and continued to stare out the window.

Bob turned off the main highway onto a dirt road that sloped downhill, passing sparse patches of tall sugar pine interlaced with a ground cover of sagebrush. At the bottom of the hill, the patches of timber gave way to wide valleys of brown grass that stretched downward to rich, green pastures of bottom land. Then the road started to level out and twist, following the riverbed. He made a turn over a bridge of heavy wooden planks that rumbled under the wheels of the pickup. Another mile brought them to the entrance of the ranch.

Bob got out of the pickup, intending to open the door for her, but she pushed it open herself and got out slowly, looking around apprehensively.

The outside of the house seemed to be suffering from neglect, and she noticed the weathered look of the faded brown cedar siding, and the cracked and peeling white trim around the windows. He opened the door, giving it a slight shove, then stepped back. She hesitated a moment, thinking he would enter first, but he surprised her by his courtesy to let her pass in front of him.

When she walked into the combined kitchen and dining room, her eyes caught sight of the boy sitting with his booted feet on the corner of an oblong dining table. He was reading a comic book. When the boy looked up and saw them, he removed his feet from the table, threw the book aside, then stood up. His wild red hair lay about his head, extending over his ears to meet a lightly freckled face.

"What's she doin' here?" he asked, coming out from behind the table.

"She's going to be staying with us for a while," Bob said. Then he added, "The doc said she'd be better here than in town."

"But she's a woman, Dad."

"I'm glad you can see that, son."

"But there hasn't been a woman livin' here since Mom died. I don't want her stayin' in **our house**."

The impact of the boy's harsh words hit her in the stomach. She glanced at Bob and saw his eyes harden.

"Stephan, you watch your manners now," Bob cautioned. "The lady is a guest in our house."

"But, Dad..." he started to protest.

"No arguments, boy. I want you to treat the lady right."

Stephan hung his head, ashamed of being corrected.

Uneasiness started to taunt her. Bob hadn't said a dozen words to her all the way to the ranch, and now his son definitely made it known that she was not welcome. "Listen, Mister Malloy," she said, "I don't think this is going to work. It's an imposition on you and your son. If you'll just take me back to town, I assure you I'll be fine."

"Can't do that. I promised the doc, and you aren't making me go back on my word. I'm not taking you back, not for a few days anyway," he finished in a stern voice.

He walked into the kitchen, drained the coffee grounds out of the pot into a sink filled with dishes, and then drew fresh water. He threw two scoops of coffee into the water and set it on the stove to boil.

"Stephan, I've got a chore to do, but I should be back before dark. While I'm gone, you stay here and fix the lady something to eat," he ordered.

"I don't want to stay here. Why can't I go with you?"

"Stephan, do like I ask. Now I told you to mind your manners."

Jan stood by, listening to the two of them, wishing she hadn't agreed to stay, but here she was, and she knew she'd have to make the best of it. He wasn't about to take her back to town, and she certainly couldn't walk.

"Why don't you take him with you? I'm really not hungry," she said. Her impression of the house also disheartened her wish to stay. The dining table was cluttered with crumbs, coffee cups and food-stained dishes. She had no idea how long they had been sitting there. Looking down into the sunken living room, she saw clothing strewn about the furniture, and saddles and tack lying on the floor. The smell of sweat from the horses filled her nostrils, causing her stomach to knot at the thought of staying in this house.

"Suit yourself," Bob said, "but the boy stays here." His statement had the ring of finality. He left the house, and Stephan didn't argue the point any further.

Stephan picked up the coffee cups and dishes and put them in the sink. Then he walked back to the table. Taking his arm, he brushed the tabletop clear of the crumbs onto the floor. "What's your name?" he finally asked stiffly.

"You can just call me Jan," she replied.

"Jan what?"

"Just Jan. I can't seem to remember my name. I can't remember anything," she explained with a forlorn expression.

"Well, you don't have to stand there. Sit down at the table, if you want," Stephan offered.

Jan heard a softening in his voice. Perhaps he noticed that she was getting disgusted with his attitude, she thought. "Thank you," she said, pulling out one of the captain chairs that surrounded the table.

"I'll bet that's scary, not bein' able to remember your name."

"Yes, it is."

"And I'll bet you lied about bein' hungry. You **are** hungry, ain't ya?"

"Yes, a little," she admitted, half smiling.

"I'll fix you something," he said, going to the kitchen and removing a kettle out of the cupboard. "Do you like beans?"

"That'll be fine," she said, hoping there would be some clean dishes.

"Dad and I like beans. We eat a lot of 'em," he said, slipping the can of beans into the electric can opener. The lid cut clean, and fell beneath the lip of the can. He pushed the lid into the beans with his fingers. Raising one edge of it, he plucked the lid free. Jan grimaced. She had noticed the blackness under his fingernails and knew his hands were not clean. She turned her head to one side, feeling her throat tighten.

"I think I'll just have some coffee," she said, changing her mind.

Paying no attention, Stephan emptied the contents of the can into the kettle and set it on the stove to cook. Steam rolled out of the coffeepot, and it started to boil. He turned the burner to simmer.

"Don't you have an electric coffee maker?" she asked, thinking what a strange way they had of making coffee.

"Naw, dad and I like it boiled. We call it hobo coffee."

"How old are you? You look a little young to be drinking coffee."

"I'm twelve years old, and I've been drinkin' coffee a long time," Stephan said, proud of the fact. Pouring her a cup of the fresh-brewed coffee, he set it in front of her.

Jan didn't know how clean the cup was, but she felt the coffee was hot enough to sterilize it. She couldn't even remember if she liked coffee. She raised the cup to her lips and sipped the hot liquid. Raising her eyebrows, she was surprised at the pleasant flavor. "This is good coffee, Stephan."

Stephan smiled. "You'll like the beans, too." He sprinkled a teaspoon full of brown sugar over them and added a chunk of butter, then stirred them until steam rolled out of the kettle. Taking two bowls from the cupboard, he filled them, then placed them on the table. Quickly grabbing a loaf of bread and two spoons from the drawer, he walked to the table and sat down.

She waited for a moment before dipping the spoon into the bowl of kidney beans. Then, blanking her mind, she started to eat. She found that she was quite hungry, and the beans were not bad tasting.

"Do you know where your father went?" she asked, not really caring, but it made conversation.

"Probably out lookin' for Old Blue."

"Who's Old Blue?"

"He's a horse," Stephan answered, shoveling a spoonful of beans into his mouth. "Dad's been trainin' him. He's goin' to race Old Blue, and he'll win, too," he informed her, not bothering to swallow before talking.

"Do you like horses?"

He gazed at her oddly, for a moment. "Sure. Don't you?"

"I don't know. I don't think I've ever been around them."

"Oh, yeah...I forgot. You can't remember. Would you like to see the horses? We got ten mares. Dad wants 'em for breedin', and we got Old Blue, Buck and my horse."

"Yes, I would like to see them."

Jan finished her bowl of beans, then picked up the dishes and put them into the sink. Stephan pulled his western hat onto his head, then noticed her shoes. Disappearing into the other room, he returned carrying a pair of boots.

"Here, put these on," he ordered. "It's pretty sloppy out there."

Jan reluctantly slipped them on. She felt foolish, running around in a pair of old dirty boots.

The sun was just above the western horizon. It would be getting dusk in another hour. Stephan directed her beyond the large barn to a fenced-in pasture. The horses were milling about aimlessly. Climbing the board fence, Jan grasped her hand on the top board to keep her balance. Stephan climbed the fence with ease and sat comfortably on top. His high-pitched whistle caught the attention of the horses. Some snorted, others whinnied, and they came toward the fence. "They think I come to feed 'em," he said.

Jan hung back from the fence. One mare approached her and stood close. She reached out to touch the animal, but it shied, dipping its head, and quickly moved away.

"Are they wild horses?" she asked.

"Heck no, they just don't know you. See that brown one with the white blaze down its face and the jet black one on the other side of the pasture?"

"Yes, I see them," she replied.

"They're the only two Thoroughbreds we have, and the rest are all Quarterhorses. All our horses are registered," he explained.

She couldn't help but note the pride in the boy's voice, and she smiled to herself while watching the horses.

"Well, they certainly are beautiful animals. Their hair is so shiny, and they're so fat."

"They ain't fat!" Stephan laughed indignantly. "They're goin' to have colts."

"Oh, I didn't know," she replied, rather embarrassed at herself.

"Well, I better feed 'em. You want to watch?"

"No, you go right ahead. I think I'll go back to the house."

Upon entering the house, her gaze fell on the mess in the kitchen. She pulled the dishes from the sink and piled them on the counter. Maybe if I tidy this place up a bit, they'll be more receptive to me, she thought. After finding all the necessary items, she started cleaning the kitchen. In twenty minutes she had the dishes cleaned and put away. Then she started cleaning the counter top and arranging the small appliances and canisters in an orderly fashion.

After wiping the dining table of the dried food particles, she noticed that papers and magazines lay haphazardly around the room. She stacked them neatly, then swept the linoleum-covered floor. She absolutely could not believe that people lived this way. 'There,' she said to herself, 'this looks a little better.'

Pouring herself another cup of coffee, she slumped into a chair. Seeing the phone on the wall, she stared at it, hoping it would ring and that the voice on the other end would somehow be recognizable. If only she could hear or see one person from her past, the mystery of who she was would be wiped away. But it was not to be. The phone didn't ring. Trying to force herself to remember was a futile exercise. She took solace in the thought that someone, somewhere, was looking for her, and through the efforts of the marshall, she would be found. She pushed the troubling questions from her mind, keeping that positive thought within her.

She started to think about Bob. The doctor had assured her that he was a good man, and that he would treat her with kindness. Well, she sure couldn't see any of those qualities in him. To her, he was a big burly man who ordered everybody around. Setting her cup in the sink, she looked through the dirty kitchen window and saw Bob and Stephan walking side by side toward the house.

When they walked into the kitchen, Stephan started rummaging through the magazines and papers she had neatly stacked.

"Hey, where's my comic book? Did you throw it away?" he demanded in a surly tone.

"Stephan, watch your attitude," Bob said, then turned to Jan. "What did you do with his book?" he asked in a demeaning voice.

While they had been alone, Jan thought Stephan's attitude had changed some, but now that his father was home, he was reverting back to his earlier behavior.

"I put his comic book in with the magazines, there in the corner. All he has to do is look for it," she said in a raised voice.

"Why didn't you just leave it out where he could find it?" Bob retorted.

Nothing was said about her efforts in making the place more presentable. All she heard was complaining about a comic book, and this infuriated her. "Look at this place!" she exclaimed, making a swoop of the room with her arm. "How can you live like this, in this filth? Don't you have any pride at all?"

Bob looked at her long and hard. "Now, hold on, lady, you got no call to be talkin' about us that way, or how we live. We're gettin' along just fine."

She could see he was angered by her remarks. His large hand was grasping the edge of the counter top, and his knuckles were white. She felt slightly frightened, but was not about to give in to it.

"Why don't you just take me back to town. I may not remember who I am or where I came from, but I know I never lived in a mess like this," she argued further.

Stephan quietly observed this strange woman and his father talking in heated discussion. He was hoping his dad would take her back to town. He was glad they were not getting along and went back to rummaging through the stack of magazines. Soon he had the magazines and papers lying in disarray again. Finally finding his book, he slouched into a chair and swung his feet onto the edge of the table.

Jan glanced in Stephan's direction. An expression of disgust crossed her face. "Look...look what your son is doing. I just cleaned off the table, and now he's got his filthy boots on it! And the magazines, **look** at them!"

Bob looked at Stephan and the mess he had made of the magazines, then noticed that the dishes were washed and the counters cleaned. Since Laura's death, keeping the house up didn't seem important anymore. He worked long, hard hours for another rancher. And, with his own interest in training his horses, there wasn't enough hours in a day to bother with housework.

Turning back to her, he could see she was near tears. He felt a twinge of guilt. He'd never acted this rudely to anyone before.

In spite of himself, he was attracted to her. Was Doctor Woodward right? Was he protecting himself and using Stephan as the vehicle? He dismissed that thought, but he knew he needed to be more considerate of her.

He finally turned to Stephan, and said, "Put your feet down, son."

"Aw, Dad."

He stared at Stephan with a firm look in his eyes. "I **said**, get your feet off the table and straighten up that pile of books."

Stephan knew he had a lot of latitude with his father, but he also knew when not to argue with him. Reluctantly, he removed his feet from the table and started stacking the books.

Jan let out a long sigh. "Thank you, both of you. If you don't mind, could you show me where I might sleep? It's been a long day, and I'm really getting tired."

"Sure, we got a spare room you can use," Bob replied, then led her down the hallway and opened the door to the room.

She entered, surprised by the orderliness and cleanliness of the bedroom. She wondered why this room had been spared the accumulation of clutter.

"This was our room before..." he started to say, then stopped abruptly. "The bathroom is right across the hall." Before closing the door behind him, she noticed a sorrowful look in his eyes.

While gazing about the room, her eyes caught sight of a photograph sitting on a nightstand beside the bed. The picture was of a man, a woman and a small child standing close together. It had to be Bob and his wife, and the boy must be Stephan, she thought. The man in the picture wore a beard, but it was short and well-groomed. The smile on his face expressed a warmth she had not yet seen, and his eyes seemed to be filled with happiness. Looking at his wife, Jan could see that she was a lovely woman. Maybe, since her death, he'd let himself become bitter, she speculated.

She placed the picture back on the nightstand, then folded the white counterpane to the foot of the bed. Digging into her paper bag, she took out her nightgown. She changed, and could hear the muffled sounds of Bob and Stephan's voices, but unable to make out what they were saying. When climbing into the bed, she found it soft and comfortable, and soon went to sleep.

Bob had reheated the leftover kidney beans and was sitting next to Stephan at the table.

"How long is she goin' to be here?" Stephan asked.

"Not long, I expect. Somebody will be looking for her."

"She's kind of uppity, ain't she, Dad?" Bob couldn't help but smile at his son's deduction of the woman. He could tell she was anything but a snob, so, if anybody was acting `uppity', it was himself, and right now he was feeling somewhat ashamed. He smiled, remembering her fiery outburst about how they lived. No woman ever had talked to him in that manner, and he found it rather appealing.

"Well, I wouldn't say that exactly. She's just got a bad situation on her hands."

"She don't care for horses, like you and me, I can tell."

"How do you know? Did you ask her?"

"I asked her if she wanted to watch me feed 'em, and she said no."

"Well, that don't mean she don't like them," he chuckled.

"Well, how about her comin' in here and takin' over, cleanin' and everything?"

Bob thought for a moment before answering. "Well now, that isn't so bad, is it? Remember how your mother kept the house. I guess we both been kinda lazy about that. Peers to me you're looking for excuses not to like her," he said, thinking maybe that's exactly what he himself was trying to do.

"You like her, Dad?"

"Don't know her, son. One day soon she'll be gone. Gone back to where she come from."

"Suppose she don't ever remember, what then? Will she stay here forever?"

"No, not hardly," Bob laughed. "I figure I'll take her into town in a couple of days and find out what the marshall has learned about her," he assured Stephan.

"Can I go with you, Dad?"

"Sure, you can. Do you want to help me over at the Monford's place tomorrow?"

"What about her?"

"She'll be okay, but right now we better turn in. Got to get an early start in the morning," he added, getting up from the table.

THREE

Jan stirred slightly and opened her eyes. Her head was throbbing. She climbed out of bed and stood before the mirror on the dresser. Pulling her hair back to view the lump on the side of her head, she raised her hand and felt it gently. The swelling had gone down some, but it was still painful. Thinking she would take one of the painkillers the doctor had given her, she reached into the pocket of her dress and took one from the container.

She had hoped that, by now, her memory would have returned, but it hadn't. Getting out of bed and making sure the robe was secured, she walked toward the kitchen.

"Good morning," she called cheerfully. There was no response. "Anybody here?" She raised her voice. Still no response. She opened the front door and looked outside. The sun was just peeking over the mountain tops to the east; it was going to be a beautiful, hot summer day, she thought. Glancing to where the pickup had been parked, she saw that it was gone.

She had the house to herself. Going into the bathroom she disrobed and climbed into the shower. The warm water eased the pain in her head, and she let its warmth flow over her body. After dressing, she went into the kitchen.

She searched for the boots Stephan had provided her. Finding them, she slipped them on and went outside. Just beyond the barn, she saw where fresh hay had been given to the horses in the pasture. "Stephan!" she yelled. She repeated his name several times. Without any response, she went back into the house, thinking he probably had gone with his father.

There was no place she could go; she was stuck here. In her mind, she felt that Doctor Woodward had her best interests at heart; what he didn't know was that Stephan wasn't accepting her situation too well. Bob had agreed with the doctor's wishes and taken her in. After last night's ordeal, he had become amiable and thoughtful to a degree, but was still rather distant. He was thrown into a situation that neither would have chosen on their own. 'Well, I'd better make the best of it,' she thought.

After eating some breakfast, she tackled the kitchen with a vengeance. When she was finished, it displayed a fresh new look.

Finding that the hard work was keeping her mind occupied, she walked into the living room, surveyed the room with hands on hips, then took a deep breath.

"What the hell can I do with this room?" she questioned aloud. She placed a load of the strewn-about clothing into the washing machine, then lugged the saddles and other tack into the garage.

While the clothes washed, she set about dusting the furniture. With a dampened mop, she wiped the hardwood floor. She looked around the living room, she couldn't help but think what a comfortable, homey atmosphere it held. Although the Early American furniture was somewhat old, it presented a fashioned look with the hardwood floor. A large, stone fireplace ran across one wall, while built-in bookcases adorned a portion of another. By the time she was done, it was mid-afternoon. She was surprised how much she had accomplished and how nice the house was looking. She wondered what Bob and Stephan's reaction would be when they came home. She hoped she wouldn't have to meet with the same confrontation as the night before.

While eating some lunch, she thought of Doctor Woodward. Perhaps he had planned this for her. He obviously was well-acquainted with Bob Malloy and his son, so he must have known how the two of them lived, and that's why he wanted her here. If keeping her busy is what he had in mind, it was working.

The buzzer sounded on the dryer, signaling that the last load of clothing was dry. After folding the clothes, she thought about taking them to their rooms, but reconsidered. That was their private domain and she didn't want to intrude. According to the way the main part of the house had looked, she only could imagine their condition.

Jan was tired of cleaning, for the moment, and decided to take a walk. Although it was getting late into the afternoon, the sun had not yet dipped behind the mountains. The dress she wore was sleeveless, and, though there was a breeze, the sun felt hot upon her arms, forming beads of sweat that moistened her skin. Approaching the barn, she entered through a small door that hung open, and she felt the cool air around her.

She looked up toward the high peak of the barn's ceiling, and streams of sunlight burst through the cracks in the siding. The air held a strange odor to her, but she imagined it smelled like any other barn. Walking on in, she saw that the center of the barn was completely open, unobstructed by beams or posts. The opposite end was so dark that it was difficult for her to see clearly. Moving a few steps further, she heard something make a loud snorting sound. She stopped abruptly and her heart started to pound. When she heard it stomp the dirt floor, she turned and ran toward the door, slamming it shut, then latching it behind her. Jan leaned against the door, trying to catch her breath. She wished that Bob were here. Her heart was still pounding, but the sanctuary of the house calmed her. She felt protected from whatever was trapped in the barn. She looked at the clock on the kitchen wall; it read seven o'clock. The sun had dropped behind the mountains, casting their shadows over the meadows.

Jan thought of Bob and Stephan. They would probably be hungry when they got home. She decided to see what they might have to prepare for dinner.

The evening shadows had darkened. Impatiently, she would gaze out the living room window where she could see the road. Soon, she saw the flickering lights of a vehicle in the distance, coming toward the house. She took the food out of the oven and set it on the table.

Upon entering the house, they immediately saw that the table was set. Bob looked at Stephan, then at Jan. He stepped further into the room, seeing the improvement in its appearance; Stephan remained quiet.

Remembering how negligent he had been the night before, Bob exclaimed, "Now **this** looks very nice, Jan, and we really appreciate it! But I don't expect you to be doing housework at all. I'm sure you're still not feeling **that** well."

"Gee, Dad, she's got dinner ready and everything," Stephan said, heading for the table.

"Ah...Stephan, wash your hands before you sit down."

Stephan stopped in mid-stride and was about to say something when he saw the stern look in his father's eyes.

"Okay," he said, plodding down the hall to the bathroom.

Bob gave Jan a sheepish look. "He's a good boy, just a little rough around the edges since his mother..."

"Yes, I've noticed," she was quick to agree.

He moved toward the table, pulled a chair to one side and was about to sit when he detected a strange look on Jan's face.

"You, too," she said.

For a moment, his steady blue eyes stared into hers. With hands on her hips, she met his gaze full on, then a faint smile spread across her face. In that brief moment, Bob saw again what a lovely woman she was and felt something he hadn't felt in some time stir within him. He said nothing, then walked to the kitchen sink, rolled up his shirt sleeves, and washed his hands.

At that moment Stephan returned to the room, plopped himself into a chair, and reached for the platter of baked chicken.

"Wait for your father to sit down, Stephan," she said in a soft voice.

Quickly drawing his hand back, he scowled at her. He was not used to this kind of treatment.

Bob took the seat at the head of the table. Jan sat across from Stephan. He slouched in his chair with his arms crossed, staring at her. Ignoring the stare, she lifted the platter of baked chicken and handed it to Bob. He, in turn, passed it to Stephan. Stephan didn't bother to use the fork she had provided. Instead, he used his fingers to put the chicken on his plate.

Jan said nothing, but his eyes made their way to hers. By the very look on his face, she knew he was conscious of making an error. He set the chicken down close to his plate, not bothering to pass the platter to her. She passed the baked potatoes to Bob, then observed Stephan pushing the plate of chicken toward her. Bob held the plate of potatoes in front of Stephan, waiting for him to take one. His eyes flitted to Jan, then he used his fork to spear the potato.

"Thank you, Stephan," she said politely. Her impression of them left much to be desired. They were both rough in their manners, especially Stephan. It was plain to see, the influence of a woman hadn't been present for some time. Still, she felt that the manners that had been there, lay just beneath the surface, and in time could be regenerated. However, she hoped she would not be there that long.

She had been alone all day, with no one to talk to, and now silence prevailed throughout the meal. She felt it would be different if she were not here. After all, she was a stranger in their home. Maybe they were shy because of that, but they need not be. She searched her mind to find something to say that would stimulate conversation. Then she remembered her trip to the barn.

"I almost forgot. There's something strange in the barn, and it scared me."

"What were you doing in the barn?" Bob asked.

"I just took a walk and ended up there. It was too dark inside to see, but I heard it growl and stomp its feet. I ran outside as fast as I could, then I closed and latched the door."

Bob laughed at her. "Probably a giant bear, or maybe a mountain lion," he said.

"Do you think so?" she asked seriously.

"Why, of course. They're always creeping into the barn. Don't know what it is them critters like about that barn." He sneaked a glance at Stephan and winked.

"Well, whatever is in that barn, it's big. I could tell by the sound of it."

"Remember that bear that got in there, Stephan?"

"Yeah, it was last week," he said, going along with the story.

"Yes, sir, he went walkin' in there, pretty as you please. This big old bear jumped me before I knew what was happenin'," he went on, while drawing his hunting knife out of its sheath. "I struggled with that old bear until I finally got this here knife out. I fought that bear and managed to get on his back, figurin' I could stick him in the belly. Well, that bear started jumpin' and buckin' like everything. It was all I could do to hang on, grabbin' fistfuls of hair."

"Oh my! Did you use you knife?" she asked, her eyes glued to him.

"Nope. He was jumpin' and buckin' so hard, I had to keep grabbin' for more hair, and it was all comin' out by the roots."

"My goodness. What happened then?"

"He's still in the barn."

"Still in...why didn't you warn me? Then, after a moment's pause, Jan asked, "Why is he still in there?"

"Ain't got no hair. He's too embarrassed to go outside."

Stephan and his father couldn't contain themselves any longer and burst out laughing. Jan knew then that she had been the victim of a joke. While she watched the two of them laugh hysterically, she couldn't help but join them. Up to this point, she had only seen the serious side of Bob, so there was no reason not to believe what he was telling her.

When their laughter had subsided Jan said, "But there **is** something in that barn."

"I'm sure there is. A rat or maybe a mountain beaver..."

"No, I am serious...go see for yourself."

"Okay," he agreed reluctantly. "Grab the twenty two, son."

Stephan pulled the gun off the gun rack above the fireplace, while Bob was finished the last bit of his dinner. He took the firearm from Stephan, and they both started for the door.

"I'm going with you!" Jan yelled, running after them.

Bob unlatched the side door where she had entered the barn earlier. Stepping inside, he reached for the light switch. "Well, I'll be damned!" he exclaimed.

Stephan and Jan entered behind him, Stephan shouted, "He's come back, Dad! Old Blue's come back!"

"You mean, that's the horse you were looking for?" she asked.

"He sure is. Throw him some hay, Stephan. We'll just leave him in for tonight."

Stephan walked to the ladder leading to the loft.

"It's a beautiful animal," Jan said. He was a deep, bluish black with a cropped main, and stood sixteen hands high. His tail raised, he pranced in circles within the large open area of the barn. She admired the sleekness of his body.

"I'm going to train him to run," Bob informed her, while moving toward the horse.

"What kind of horse is it?" she asked, following behind him. She remembered that Stephan had pointed out the Thoroughbreds and Quarter Horses, but she didn't know one from the other.

"He's a Quarter Horse," he replied.

"You'll have to explain that to me one day."

He reached for a short rope which hung by a nail along the wall. Slowly approaching Old Blue, he slipped the rope around his neck and formed a rope halter which he placed over his head. Bob clucked at the horse while jerking lightly on the end of the rope. Blue backed a step, with his ears pricked, then stood perfectly still.

"How old is he?"

"He'll be two years old next January. That's when I'll start training him to run," Bob replied. He leaped across the horse's back, then swiftly moved his body to a sitting position.

Jan was surprised by his supple, athletic quickness. He sat upright, gracefully wheeling the animal in a circle. In these quiet moments, she took a long look at the man she was staying with. Bob's broad chest tapered to a small waist, his lean legs hugging Old Blue. She felt her stomach flutter at the site of him sitting so tall and proud on the horse. Old Blue moved swiftly to his commands, and she thought Bob looked a part of the animal.

Raising his leg over the withers, he slid to the ground and rubbed his hands over the horse's neck and back with affection, while speaking in soft, gentle tones. Jan stood watching this rugged, bushy-bearded man exhibit a gentleness she thought could not exist in him. But it did, and she felt an admiration for him.

"Would you like to sit on him?" he asked, interrupting her thoughts.

"No thanks. I can't afford to let you ruin another dress," she replied, smiling.

She saw his shaggy beard part into a smile, exhibiting gleaming white teeth. She also noticed his blue eyes become soft when he smiled. "Sorry about that. We'll have to get you some jeans or pants to wear."

"It isn't necessary. I'm just thankful you found me when you did." His gaze steadied on her, and she sensed a slight warming in her cheeks. She looked away, wondering why she felt this sudden sensation.

Stephan rolled a bale of hay off the loft onto the dirt floor. It burst apart when it hit the ground, breaking the awkwardness of the moment.

"Pick up that wire, son. We don't want him getting tangled in it," he ordered while holding onto Blue.

Stephan climbed from the loft and picked up the wire as he walked toward them.

Bob slipped the rope halter over Blue's nose and watched as the horse dipped his head, then quickly darted for the hay. After making sure Old Blue was secure for the night, the three of them left the barn.

Inside, Jan started to clear the table, and Bob assisted by removing the plates and silverware. She placed the leftover food in the refrigerator, then took a clean cup, poured it to the brim with coffee, and handed it to him.

Stephan sat watching the two of them. Seeing his father helping her brought flashes of the past into his memory, and it angered and hurt him. He remembered how his father used to help his mother after an evening meal. But his mother was gone, and that was a long time ago. Why, all of a sudden, was he helping her? Just because she was a pretty woman, or was he beginning to like her?

Stephan was confused. Neither of them had even looked his way. They seemed too occupied with each other. Without a word to either of them, he slipped quietly into his bedroom.

Jan filled the sink with hot, soapy water and started washing the dishes. Bob grabbed a towel and started to dry them. Suddenly feeling uncomfortable by having him so near, she said, "Why don't you relax and drink your coffee before it gets cold."

"You can wash and I'll dry," he replied.

"If you don't mind, I'd prefer to let them air-dry," she replied curtly.

"Well, okay, if you insist," he said, throwing the towel onto the counter.

While Bob glanced at her washing the dishes, he started to remember an earlier time in his life. Because of her presence and the touch she had placed on his home, he became painfully aware of his wife. Laura had filled their home with love, and now this woman who he knew nothing about, was making her presence felt.

The aroused feelings he felt before were again present. The growing attraction for this woman confused him. Why should he have these feelings? Was he feeling sorry for her, or was it just because he felt a need for female companionship? He shook his head. This is ridiculous, she's been here less than two days, he thought. He couldn't allow himself these feelings. She would be out of his life. Most likely someone would come for her, or her memory returned.

She put the last dish into the rack to drain, poured herself a cup of coffee, and joined him.

"Where's Stephan?" she asked.

Bob looked around realizing that Stephan wasn't in the room. "Probably tired. He worked pretty hard today. More than likely went to bed," he replied.

She sipped at her coffee, creating a moment of silence. Again, there was an awkwardness between them, and they both started to say something at once. "I'm sorry; you go first," he said, smiling.

"Oh, I was just going to say I noticed a picture, apparently a family picture, in the bedroom, and I was wondering about it."

"Yes. It's of my wife and I with Stephan. He was four when that was taken."

"Your wife was a beautiful woman."

"Thank you. She **was** beautiful and a good wife and mother."

She saw the hurt still lingering in his eyes at her mention. "I'm sorry," she said, feeling compassion for him.

"It's one of those things that happen, but it's been especially hard on Stephan. He was very attached to his mother," he explained. He avoided eye contact with her, first looking at the ceiling, then shifting to the living room almost like something there had caught his attention.

She sensed he would have been embarrassed had he not been able to conceal the emotion he felt filling his eyes. And, in that moment, she knew he must have loved his wife very much.

"What were you going to say to me?" she asked, changing the conversation.

"Ah...I was just going to ask if you have any recollection of anything?"

"No, my mind is a complete blank, and it worries me."

"Doc said your memory may come back to you in a few days."

"I hope so. I have no idea who I am, or why I'm here. I feel so alone and empty. I keep hoping and trying to think, but I can't remember anything." She gazed into his eyes and saw a hint of understanding in them.

"Well, I don't think you've forgotten everything. That chicken was real tasty. If you forgot everything, how'd you remember to do that?"

She smiled at the compliment. "Thank you, but I don't know how I did it. I just cooked it."

"Kinda like automatic, you just knew?"

"Yes, I suppose."

"That could be a good sign, couldn't it? Maybe, with some time, your memory will slowly return," he said, trying to lift her spirits.

"But how much time will it take? I can't stay here forever."

"This is only your second day. It'll just take some time."

Strange, she thought, watching and listening to him, this tall, broad-shouldered, and seemingly rough man, exhibited a tenderness in his eyes and in his voice that belied his appearance. Perhaps it was his shaggy beard or his initial gruffness that had formed her first opinion, but at the present, she found herself becoming more at ease with him.

"Not too long, I hope. I want you to know I appreciate everything being done for me by you and the doctor. Without your help, I'd be lost."

Bob could see the confusion and fear in her eyes and he felt her anxiety. But, despite what he saw in this fleeting moment, he had experienced a strength in her that tugged at him. He felt it would only be a matter of time and she would remember everything.

She had cleaned much of the house and also had shown some control over Stephan. It had been just the two of them, but with her presence on the scene, he got a glimpse at the lack of direction he was giving the boy. His good sense told him that change was in the air.

"Maybe this situation will work out for the both of us."

"What do you mean?" she asked, puzzled by his statement.

"Well, I was thinking. Being as how it may take some time to locate someone who knows who you are, you're welcome to stay here as long as it takes. I see how you are with Stephan, and I'm thinking, a woman's hand around here ain't such a bad thing."

"I have a feeling that the boy resents my being here."

"He's just not used to having a woman around since his mother passed away. Like I said, he's a little rough around the edges, but maybe you could smooth them out a little."

"You saw him at dinner tonight. He just glared at me with pure anger in his eyes."

"Yep, I saw that, but you handled it well. You also did a fine job of puttin' this house back in order, and I appreciate it."

"There's still a lot to do, I'm afraid," she replied, feeling somewhat proud that he had noticed.

"Do we have a deal then?"

She sat thinking for a moment. She had walked into a disorganized, dirty house. Her first impulse had been to leave, but, looking at what she had done with the house thus far, she could see this home better place to stay than an orderly but lonely room in town.

When Bob had first found her, his manner seemed indifferent and brusque. He felt obligated to help her because he had found her alone and confused. However, after talking with him, she sensed that he was trying to comfort her and make her feel welcome.

"I've caused you a lot of trouble, Bob, and I'm sorry. If I have to stay here for awhile, the least I can do is cook for you and Stephan and keep up the house. But just until something happens," she added.

"Thank you, Jan," he replied warmly.

"There isn't much food in the house. You'll have to do some shopping."

"We'll all go into town tomorrow. You can pick up whatever we need, and we'll get you those new clothes I promised," he said, then smiled.

Jan returned his smile warmly, and their eyes met for a brief moment. Feeling an instant flutter of excitement, she quickly glanced away. The moment caught her off guard. She rose from the table, and cleared her throat in an effort to cover this sudden feeling. "Well, it's getting late, good night, Bob."

"Yep, it's that time again. See you in the morning, Jan."

He stared after her while she walked down the hallway and into her room, then took a deep breath. He, too, had sensed the moment excitement.

FOUR

The pickup rolled along the dusty, dirt road toward the main highway leading to Winthrop. Bob was concerned over Stephan's refusal to make the trip into town. On other occasions, he would have been disappointed not going. They pulled onto the main road, Bob mentioned it, shaking his head.

"I told you he resents me," Jan replied, remembering the boy's reaction when he heard she was going along.

"Well, if he does, I'm going to have a talk with that young man."

The statement surprised her. Last evening Bob had defended Stephan's mannerisms, saying he was a little rough around the edges. Now she had the impression that he would not tolerate any insolence toward her, and she wondered about his change in attitude. "Why don't you just let it go? If you make an issue of it, you'll only put me between the two of you, and I don't want that."

"Jan, this has happened before. I've seen this type of reaction around others. He has to learn that there's more than just the two of us now, at least for a little while."

"You mean, he's reacted this way with other women?"

"More or less, but in a subtle way. He was extremely close to his mother, and now he has attached that closeness to me."

"That's perfectly understandable; you're his father."

"In a way I feel that's not healthy for him. Whenever I bring lady friends to the ranch, maybe for a day of horseback riding or just to visit, he gets very quiet and keeps to himself. Later he'll ask all kinds of questions about them. I can see he doesn't want them around, or me around them."

"I think I'm beginning to understand. He doesn't want another woman taking his mother's place."

"I think you have a handle on it. I've tried to reassure him that it's not going to happen, and I've purposely avoided any serious relationships for that reason."

"But you **do** have lady friends?" she asked hesitantly.

"A couple, but, like I said, nothing serious. I've known them for quite some time, even before Laura...passed on."

She felt a sudden relief that he had no on-going relationships with any woman. This is silly, she thought. Why should I care if he has a girlfriend? I don't even know this man. "Perhaps when he's older he'll understand."

"I'm hoping he will," Bob replied.

It had been some time since he felt at ease with a woman, but, with Jan it was different. Perhaps he felt that sense of ease because she seemed genuinely interested in what he had to say.

Though he kept his eyes on the road, he couldn't help stealing glances at her from the corner of his eye. Her auburn hair shimmered in the sunlight streaming into the truck. He began to feel the same stirring he had felt the night before, and quickly admonished himself for it.

He had no right to these feelings; he knew nothing about her. Doctor Woodward had noticed the same sophisticated aura in her. Maybe it meant nothing, but she had a life before he had found her. She may be a married woman and could have children.

"Do you have any other family besides Stephan?" she asked.

"Yes, I do, but they all live in Los Angeles. My father and two older brothers own a large, very lucrative engineering firm, but that was never my thing. Horses were always my first love, and my parents could never understand my dream of owning a ranch. I always felt like the oddball of the family. At their insistence, and trying to make them happy, I went to college and got an engineering degree and joined the firm, but I was suffocating. I just felt like I had to get away, so I moved to Seattle. I didn't have much money to buy a ranch right off, and I wasn't about to take any from my parents, so I went to work for the Honeywell Corporation. That's where I met Laura. She shared my dream, and we saved every penny we could, then bought the ranch."

He looked at Jan and smiled. "I'm afraid I've probably bored you to death."

"No, you haven't in the least," she replied, returning his smile. "Do your parents ever come to visit you and Stephan?"

"Oh, about two years ago they came to stay for a week, but things were so strained between us, they left after only two days."

She was saddened by the story, and felt that it wasn't any wonder Stephan was so attached to his father; he had no one else.

Stephan remained in his room until he heard the pickup pull out of the driveway. The memory of watching his father help Jan the night before still angered him. He refused to accompany them to town, wanting to be alone to think.

The image of his mother became vivid in his mind. No one could possibly replace her. Yet his father seemed to be searching for that very thing. He could not understand why his father would even **consider** another woman in their house, and he felt that in the past, he had successfully prevented this from happening. Now, because of these unusual circumstances, there was not only a woman living with them, but a total stranger.

This woman is going to ruin everything, he thought. His father and he were getting along just fine the way they were. He felt they didn't need anybody but each other. So what if the house wasn't neat and clean and orderly; whose business was it anyway?

He remembered how it was when his mother was alive; she had always kept the house in good order, and there was always a piping hot meal waiting for them. He could still see his mother's smiling face when they talked about the day's events. She loved the horses and the ranch, but that was all gone now. It could never be the same again. 'And now this strange woman, from out of nowhere, takes over and does what she wants. Nobody asked her to do these things.'

It was ten o'clock when Bob pulled the pickup to a stop in front of Winthrop's one and only general store. When he had brought her to see Doctor Woodward, she had paid no attention to her surroundings. She got out of the pickup and waited for Bob, and noticed the false-fronted buildings and the wooden sidewalks, which lined the single road running through town. She stood still, taking it all in, as though mesmerized by what she saw. A flash of a road sign reading the town's name quickly flickered through her mind, but it was gone.

Bob walked toward her, he could see that her mind was occupied. "Are you okay?" he asked with concern.

His voice broke her preoccupation and she replied, "Oh, yes, I'm fine."

"You looked kinda lost there for a minute."

"This town seems strange to me."

"Well, you didn't get to see much of it except the doc's office."

"I wasn't meaning the size of the town or the western appearance. It's like there's something in my memory that I can't quite grasp...that makes it strange. I just can't remember..."

Seeing the sadness in her eyes and wanting to comfort her, Bob gently put his arm around her.

"Don't worry about it, Jan. Maybe little bits and pieces are starting to come back. Just give it more time."

With the tingling, warming strength of his arm and the soft, confident look in his eyes, she started to feel reassured.

"Can we go to the marshall's office?" she asked anxiously. "Maybe he's received some information," He smiled down at her. "Sure we can, but there's plenty of time for that." He didn't bother to remove his arm from her, and gently directed her toward the general store.

Inside, the storekeeper's wife saw Bob and Jan enter and immediately came from behind the counter to greet them.

"Hi, Bob. This must be the poor, dear girl you found," she noted, looking at Jan with a concerned expression.

Bob turned to Jan with a slight grin on his face. "I'm afraid, with Winthrop being as small as it is, news gets around town pretty fast. This is Jan," he said, introducing her. "And, Jan, this is Molly. She and her husband Fred own this store."

"Of course, news travels fast. Everybody knows everybody and everything that goes on in town. How are you feeling, dear?" Molly asked.

Molly was well into her later years. Her graying hair, which was cut short above her ears and parted on the side, lay straight. She smiled easily and her warm interest seemed genuine. She wore a one-piece dark green dress that hung three inches below the knees and covered her slightly overweight frame.

"I'm feeling just fine. Thank you for asking," Jan replied.

"That's a terrible bruise," Molly said, observing the discolored yellowish mark on the side of her head.

Jan placed her hand to where the lump was located and felt it. "It's still a little tender, but not as painful as it was."

"We need to get her some clothes, Molly," Bob interjected.

"Certainly. What did you have in mind?"

"Some jeans and shirts," he informed her.

"They're back here," Molly said, motioning for Jan to follow. Her battered tennis shoes squeaked on the old wooden floor. Bob started to follow, but Molly stopped him.

"I'll help her. Besides, she has to try them on. Now you just go on and amuse yourself while I get her fixed up."

Forty-five minutes had passed before Molly and Jan appeared at the counter with the selected apparel. Jan had discarded the dress she was wearing, and now stood before Bob in blue jeans that were molded to her trim hips. The stove-pipe legs were slipped over dark tan western boots and snugly fit her shapely thighs. The western-cut shirt was tucked tightly within the waistband of the jeans and stretched over her rounded breasts, accentuating them. Jan looked at Bob, then pirouetted. She set the items on the counter and noted the approval of her appearance in Bob's eyes. "Do I look acceptable in these clothes?" she asked, wanting confirmation of the approval she had seen. "Yep, you look okay," he said, his eyes darting between the two women.

Jan had hoped for a stronger affirmation, but, watching his eyes, she sensed his embarrassment. Molly smiled, for she, too, had sensed it.

"You want these on your bill, Bob?"

"Yes, please," he replied.

"Thank you, Bob. I appreciate your doing this for me."

"It's all right, Jan; you'll be working it off," he joked.

Molly raised her eyebrows and smiled slyly. Bob could see the implication of his remark on Molly's face and quickly corrected himself.

"You know what I mean. Doing housework and stuff like that," he stammered.

Jan chuckled at his attempt to clarify his meaning to Molly. Despite the humor of this innocent moment, it gave her more insight to the sensitivity of this rugged man.

Molly slipped the clothing into a large plastic bag, then indicated to Bob that she would add them to his account. Thanking Molly for her assistance, they left the general store and proceeded to the marshall's office.

Marshall Dan Miller was sitting at his small desk reading the Seattle Post. He was in his late forties with premature gray hair and was a bit on the portly side. Even though it was the tourist season, Marshall Miller's activity didn't increase significantly; however, he did dignify the presence of law and order. He lay the paper to one side when Bob and Jan entered the office.

"Morning, Dan. We thought we'd stop in and see if you've heard anything."

"Not yet," the marshall responded Bob glanced at Jan and saw the disappointment in her expression. "Is there anything more we can do?"

"I don't know that there's anything you can do but wait it out for a while. I sent her fingerprints and photograph to the Department of Vital Statistics in Seattle. If they can make a match with her prints, we'll know who she is."

"Suppose she's never been fingerprinted, what then?"

Dan shrugged. "Just hope that someone recognizes her photograph. "He let his gaze rest on Jan. "Have you remembered anything that can help us?" he asked.

"No, I'm at a total loss."

"I guess our hands are tied, unless you happen to remember something that'll give me more to go on."

"Right now I'm afraid I can't do that," she said, walking away. She gazed out the window, fighting to hold back the tears. How could just a simple bump on the head cause her to lose all remembrance of the past? Was she mentally blocking something out? She closed her eyes tightly, bent on remembering, but, no matter how hard she tried, nothing came to her. Nothing. Her mind was blank.

Feeling sorry for herself wouldn't help anything. She had to keep thinking the marshall would hear some news, and someone who cared about her would be coming.

Dan sat watching her. He knew there was nothing he could say, or do in a comforting way. An awkward silence prevailed for the moment, then he broke the silence by turning his attention to Bob.

"Doc tells me Old Blue got away."

"Yep, came back on his own, though," Bob replied, watching Jan. He sensed her distress, and knew she was trying to compose herself.

"I think he's going to be a good one. When you going to start training him for the big race?"

He was finding it hard to concentrate on what Dan was saying. "Ah...we'll be starting soon."

"Oh, are you going to let Stephan help train him?" the marshall asked.

He moved to Jan's side. "Yeah. He's about the right age, and a pretty good hand with the horses. I know he'll enjoy it."

"Well, I wish you luck with Blue."

"Thanks, Dan," Bob said, guiding Jan to the door.

Once they were outside in the sunlight, her misty eyes, but he couldn't begin to imagine her feelings. He wanted to do something to change the mood. He looked at his watch. "Darn near noon. You getting hungry?"

"I can fix us something at home," she replied.

"Heck, we're in town. Let's go to Three Fingered Jack's and get a bite."

Finding it hard to turn down his invitation, she replied, "I'm with you."

Three Fingered Jack's was a combination restaurant and saloon. They entered through the saloon portion and walked toward the restaurant. The atmosphere was in keeping with western tradition. Stuffed deer and elk heads decorated the walls, and large mirrors ran behind the length of the bar. After a quick lunch and some relaxed conversation mixed with humor, her spirits had been lifted.

August was coming to a close. Stephan had been working with his father at the Monford ranch, barning the last cutting of timothy and alfalfa that had been bailed.

With each passing day, Stephan saw continued improvement in the home environment, and deep within himself, he could not deny the pleasure of a changed atmosphere. In part, she was affecting the lazy attitude he had come to portray since the passing of his mother. She was even conditioning his lack of manners, and, though this gave rise to defiance, he did not show it outwardly.

He had hoped with each new day there would be some word of someone coming for her. He would listen intently to the talk between this woman and his father, but detected nothing in their conversations to warrant his feeling that there was an attraction between them. It was mostly immaterial things they discussed. However, it was the subtle glances toward each other that worried him. In that regard, he saw a difference in his father he had not observed with his other women friends. It created a fear in him, a fear that his mother would be forgotten.

On their last day of work, they were all sitting at the table, enjoying one of Jan's delicious dinners. when Bob announced,

"We're going to be pretty busy around here this next week; we got a lot of hay to get out of the fields for ourselves."

"We goin' to have any help this year, Dad?" Stephan asked.

"Monford agreed to let me use his new harrowbed. I figured I'd hire a couple of boys to help barn the hay. That way you won't have to work as hard as you did last year," Bob said, poking Stephan in the ribs.

"What's a harrowbed?" Jan asked, looking at Stephan.

"It's a machine that picks up the bales of hay. When the bed gets full you drive it to the barn and dump it. Cut's out some extra help and it's faster," Stephan replied, then turned to Bob and excitedly asked, "Can I drive it, Dad?"

"I don't know. It's a pretty expensive piece of equipment."

"I drove the tractor, and I've even drove the windrower," Stephan pleaded his case.

"We'll see, son. We got a week to get the work done before you go back to school."

"School, yuk!" Stephan exclaimed with a sour look on his face.

"Don't you like school, Stephan?" Jan asked seriously.

"It's okay, I guess."

At the mention of the word 'school', vague memories started to filter through her mind of a time long ago. She rose from the table and started clearing it. Bob assisted her in his usual way. Later, she sat on the porch staring up into the starry night, she tried to concentrate on the bits and pieces of those memories, but they were only flashing images.

Bob stood at the door a moment, observing her, then pushed the door open and stepped onto the porch. "You looked like you were a million miles from here," he noted.

Jan gazed up into his gentle eyes and smiled. "I guess I was, for a moment."

"What were you thinking about?"

"Oh, just trying to figure out who I am and where I belong."

He looked down at her, seeing the sadness in her emerald green eyes. He found himself growing fonder of this beautiful woman with each passing day, and he noticed that a happiness had settled inside him that had not been there for quite some time. He knew it was because of her. He also knew that he shouldn't be having these feelings towards her. She had a life somewhere else.

He wished he could do something more to help her, but, for right now, all he could do was try to comfort her. He sat down on the stoop next to her.

"Don't worry, Jan, your memory will come back. It's only been a few weeks. Maybe it's just going to take a little longer than we thought. You have to keep thinking positively." He started to cover her hand with his, but Stephan came bounding out the door.

"I'm going to feed the stock, since you seem to be so busy," he said in a harsh tone when he passed them.

"Stephan's attitude is another concern. I feel my being here has only put a gap between you two. He's so quiet and aloof. I can see he still doesn't want me here."

"Maybe you're being too sensitive. After all, he's just a boy."

"I don't think I'm being overly sensitive," she said impatiently. "That boy still resents me. I just wish there was something I could do to make him like me."

"He'll come around. At least you've taught him some table manners, and he's keeping his feet off the table," Bob said, then laughed.

Even though Stephan acted cold towards her, Jan liked and respected him. He was a hard worker who never asked for much in return. In her mind, for some unexplained reason, she could relate to the loss of his mother at such a young age.

"What day does school start?"

"Well, Labor Day is this weekend. It's a three-day holiday, and there's always a big celebration in town, then it starts on Tuesday," Bob answered.

"He'll be needing new clothes for school, won't he?" Jan asked.

"Yeah, he will, and I had a thought about that."

"What thought?"

"You taking Stephan school shopping. Maybe being alone together might change things."

"Suppose he doesn't want to go with me?"

"I'll make some excuse why I can't take him."

"And you think that'll make a difference?"

"It can't hurt. Take him on Friday, okay?" he said and stood up. "Well, guess I'll give Stephan a hand with the stock."

Her eyes followed him while he walked off toward the barn. There was something about this man that made her heart flutter whenever he looked at her.

She watched the horses in the moonlight and smiled to herself. They were running after each other, as if playing a game of tag. In this peaceful moment, a contentment filled her soul.

FIVE

The following morning, Bob and Stephan had just finished eating and were heading outside when Monford pulled in with the harrowbed, followed by a pickup. Jan stood at the window watching while the two men talked to each other. Then she watched Stephan and his father climb onto the seat of the harrowbed and head for the fields.

She returned to the task of tidying the kitchen and other household chores that had become so much a part of her life here. Periodically she could hear the whine of the harrowbed engine nearing the barn to deliver a load of hay.

The midmorning sun was pouring its relentless heat over the landscape when Stephan entered the house. His bare chest was wet with sweat and chaff from the hay on his sticky body. Grabbing a glass from the cupboard, he turned the faucet, letting the water run until it got cold, then gulped the water from the glass.

"We need some cold water for the guys," he said in his usual rough tone.

"Would you like me to make some lemonade?" she offered.

"Yeah. Will you bring it out to us?"

"Sure."

Jan delivered a gallon thermos of lemonade to the barn. She saw that Stephan and a man were working in the loft. Another man was lifting bales onto an elevator which extended from the ground to the loft above. Looking around and not seeing Bob, she assumed that he was in the field. When the man lifting the bales saw her, he shut down the elevator. "Break time!" he shouted. Then he smiled when she handed him a cup.

Climbing down from the loft, Stephan introduced the two men to her. The man loading the elevator was Jeff Riggs and the man with Stephan was Bill Holt. She filled their cups, her eyes noticing the broad smile, the tussled sandy hair, and the unmistakable steady, unwavering gaze of Bill's eyes upon her.

She felt her face flush with embarrassment. She recapped the thermos and set it in the shade.

"Let me know when you run out, Stephan." Heading away from them, she could still feel the man's eyes following her.

When she was out of earshot, Bill said, "She's one good-lookin' lady. Never seen her before. Where'd your Dad meet her?"

Stephan explained the circumstances surrounding Jan, then, while they continued to work, Bill occasionally would mention her name and ask pointed questions about her.

Stephan noticed that Bill's attention had been glued to her the whole time she was serving the lemonade. He also noticed the blush which had crossed her face.

"I think she likes you, Bill," Stephan said, nudging him on the arm.

"Oh, she didn't even look at me," he retorted.

"I saw her face get all red. That must mean somethin'."

"Yeah, what? I didn't see her face get red."

"Well, it did," Stephan argued. "Do you like her, Bill?"

"She's a good-looking woman, yeah, I like her," he admitted.

"Why don't you ask her to the dance Saturday night? Bet she'd like to go," Stephan suggested.

"Are you crazy, kid! She's living with your dad."

"No, she ain't," Stephan was quick to respond in a rising voice. "She's just stayin' with us until she gets better."

"Better? I don't see anything wrong with **that** woman," Bill noted with a lustful look on his face.

"You know what I mean. I told you."

"If I was to ask her, bet your dad would have something to say about it."

"She don't mean nothing to my dad. But, if you're afraid..."

"Afraid!" Bill laughed, looking away.

"You are afraid," Stephan teased, then started parading around and clucking like a chicken.

"Okay, by God," Bill said, angered by Stephan's teasing, "I **will** ask her to go to the dance."

Stephan smiled mischievously. He was pleased with himself, because he had successfully goaded Bill into asking her out.

In his mind, he could see Bill actively pursuing her, and in doing so, distancing the interest he saw in his father toward her.

It was approaching two o'clock in the afternoon when Bill called for a break. The barn was hot and the physical activity of hoisting bales into place caused them to sweat profusely. Climbing down from the loft, Bill uncapped the thermos, but it was empty.

"How about getting her to refill this?" he asked, holding the thermos out to Stephan.

Stephan reached out instinctively, then drew his hand back and plopped on the ground.

"You do it. I'm too tired," he said, knowing this was an opportunity for Bill to be alone with Jan.

Bill didn't hesitate in leaving Jeff and Stephan to relax. He approached the house and knocked on the door, then opened it. Jan was sitting at the table mending one of Stephan's shirts.

"Pardon me, ma'am, but could we get some more lemonade?"

"Certainly, come on in and sit down," she invited with a pleasant smile.

Bill positioned himself at the table. Jan could feel his eyes follow her, and it was making her feel uncomfortable.

"It must be pretty hot out there," she said, attempting to make conversation.

"It sure is, 'specially when you're workin' in it."

"Is it always this hot in the summer?"

"Yeah, but after Labor Day it starts to get cooler," he said.

"I understand there's a celebration in town this weekend."

He couldn't have hoped for a better lead-in. "Yeah, there's dancin' and partyin' all weekend. Are you goin'?"

"I hadn't even thought about it," she replied.

"Has Bob said anything about goin'?"

Bob hadn't mentioned anything about the holiday celebration except for the fact it was that weekend. She wondered if he had plans to join in the activities. "No. I don't know if he plans to or not," she finally answered.

"Well, I would be right pleased to take you to the dance...if you'd like to go."

His sudden invitation caught her off guard. He was obviously interested in her, and was taking this opportunity to ask her out. After capping the thermos of lemonade, she set it on the table. "It could be fun, I suppose, but I don't think so."

He thought he heard a sign of uncertainty in her words. "Think about it, and I'll check with you later, okay?" Without waiting for an answer he grabbed the thermos and hurriedly left the house.

Yes, she would like to participate in the coming celebration, she told herself. In all the time she'd been here, she'd only been to town twice. Although Bob had said nothing concerning the weekend, there was still plenty of time. She had to admit to herself that she would much rather attend the dance with Bob.

After breakfast on Friday morning, Jan hesitantly mentioned going to town. "Do you know what we're going to do today, Stephan?" she asked, trying to be optimistic.

"What?" he responded with a puzzled look.

"We're going shopping."

"What for?"

"Well, I thought it would be nice to get you some new clothes. It'll be the last chance before school starts."

He shot a quick glance toward his father. "Are you goin' along, Dad?"

"Nope, not this time, son. Just you and Jan."

"I don't need any new clothes. I don't wanta go."

Bob glanced at Jan and saw the disappointment on her face. "Listen, son. I'd take you, like always, but Monford is coming for his equipment and I gotta be here. Now I want you to go with Jan, and no argument," he said forcefully.

When his father talked in those tones, Stephan knew better than to persist. He was also disappointed that his plan involving

Bill and Jan had not worked out. There was nothing he could do about that, or his father not going to town.

Jan pulled the pickup to a stop in front of the general store. Molly spotted them when they entered and come bustling from behind the counter to greet them.

"How are things at the ranch?" she asked.

"Keeping busy. Stephan has really been working hard helping his father," she said, glancing at him.

"And how are you...anything?"

Jan shook her head negatively, understanding her question. Then, not wanting to talk about her memory loss, she announced, "We're here to do some school shopping for Stephan."

"What am I going to get?" he asked.

"Well, let's see. What does your father usually get you?"

"Some new shirts and pants. Sometimes a new pair of boots," he said quietly, shyly.

Molly escorted them to the section containing boys clothing, then left them to each other. An hour passed before they returned to the counter. Between the two of them their arms were loaded with clothing.

"It looks like you went all out. Will this be cash or charge?" Molly asked.

"Cash, Molly. Mister Malloy said to pay for the things I got the other day, too."

"Wish all my customers were as eager to pay their bill as Bob," Molly mumbled as she sifted through her accounts. Finding Bob's, she pulled it from the file, then began totaling the items.

"That comes to two hundred thirty-eight dollars and twenty-two cents," she declared.

Jan reached into her pocket and withdrew the folded currency Bob had given her, then handed Molly three crisp one hundred dollar bills. After leaving the store, they carried the packages to the pickup. "Are you getting hungry, Stephan?" Jan asked.

"A little," he answered, with his head hanging down. He had hoped they would be leaving to go back to the ranch, but now she wanted him to eat with her.

"Shall we go to Three Fingered Jack's? That's a good place to eat."

"Yeah, and they have an arcade..." he replied, his spirits beginning to lift, then suddenly the excitement in his eyes disappeared.

"You didn't bring any money, did you?" she asked.

"No, I forgot to, but that's okay."

They entered the restaurant and ordered hamburgers, fries and milk shakes. When the food was delivered, she handed the waitress two one-dollar bills and asked her to change them for quarters.

"You didn't have to do that," Stephan said.

"You like to play the machines, don't you?"

"Yeah, my dad always lets me play when we come to town."

"Well, why should it be any different now? It's his money. He just couldn't come to town today." She chuckled, hoping Stephan would see the humor in her words.

The waitress returned with the quarters and Jan shoved them in front of him.

"Can I take my food with me?" he asked sheepishly, expecting her to say no.

"Sure, you can."

Stephan slid out of the booth with his food. After taking a few steps, he stopped and turned. "Do you want to come with me?" "No. I'll be just fine right here."

She watched him walking toward the arcade room, thinking she had made some progress in their relationship. She remembered the first time they were alone together. His attitude was impetuous in the beginning, but, eventually he had softened. It started that way this morning, and now he seemed to be softening again. Perhaps, with time, she thought, things will improve between them.

Her thoughts were interrupted by a man's voice. She looked up and saw Bill Holt standing beside her.

"I just came in to get a bite to eat and saw you sitting here. May I join you?" he asked.

"Sure," she said as he sat down across from her.

"Are you here...alone?" he asked guardedly.

"Are you asking if Mister Malloy is in town?" She smiled, noticing his cautious tone.

"Well, I don't know... is he?"

"No, I brought Stephan in to do some school shopping. He's in the back room right now playing the machines."

"I haven't had the chance to ask you if you've made up your mind about Saturday night."

"Made up my mind? I don't recall that I was supposed to. If you remember right, I said I didn't think so."

"But, you did say you thought it might be fun," he reminded her.

"I'm sure it would be."

"Has Bob asked you to the dance?"

"He hasn't said a word about it. I assume he's not going."

"Well, then the offer's still open. The town will be hoppin'. You really shouldn't miss it," he added, grinning.

She took a bite of the sandwich and chewed slowly, using the time to think rather than talk. Through their daily contact and conversations she found Bob to be kind, thoughtful and sensitive. Under his scraggly beard and unruly hair, he encompassed a ruggedness that attracted her to him, though she didn't know why.

She was not unaware of the stolen appreciative glances he bestowed upon her. There were no words between them to indicate any such attraction, but she felt that it existed for him as much as it did for her. Perhaps because of Stephan's attitude he was hesitant to ask her to join in the weekend festivities, and she could understand this, to a point.

Once again she let her mind reflect on his fleeting glances when he thought she wasn't looking. If he had any attraction to her, going to the dance with Bill, may have some positive effect in moving him in her direction. "You know, you're right. I shouldn't miss it."

"You mean, you'll go out with me?" Bill was surprised at her sudden turn-around. "That's great, Jan! What time shall I pick you up?"

"Are you sure you want to do this? It's a long trip back and forth to the ranch."

"From where I'm sitting, you're worth every mile of it," he said with an appreciative look.

She blushed at the compliment, but felt uneasy with herself for impulsively accepting his invitation. Just because Bob apparently didn't want to ask her to the dance didn't mean that she had to go with the first man who asked her.

"Shall we say, around seven-thirty or eight o'clock?" he asked, interrupting her thoughts.

"That'll be fine," she replied reluctantly.

"Well, I think I'll go see Stephan before you leave for home. And I'll see you before eight tomorrow night."

Bill found Stephan at one of the machines and tapped him on the shoulder. "Hey, little buddy, I just wanted to thank you for putting me on to Jan. She's going to the dance with me tomorrow night."

"Hey, that's great. I told you she liked you," Stephan said, not taking his eyes off the screen.

"She's a great looker. Wait till the boys see me with her. They'll be drooling in their beer," he said with a broad grin.

"Yeah, she's okay."

Bill laughed at Stephan's immaturity, remembering his own at his age. "Well, kid, I gotta' go. See ya later, right?"

"Right," Stephan returned, still keeping his eyes on the screen. The game finally ended and so did the quarters Jan had given him. He walked out into the restaurant and took his seat.

"Did you see Bill?" she asked, wondering if Bill had mentioned that he was taking her to the dance.

"Yeah, I saw him," he replied curtly.

"What did he want to see you about?"

"Nothing important. He just wanted to say hi and see if dad needed anymore help," he lied.

If Stephan knew she was going to the dance with Bill, he gave no hint of it, she thought to herself. "Are you ready to head back, pardner?"

Stephan couldn't help but laugh at her attempt at a western drawl. "Yep," he answered, sliding out of the booth.

After Stephan and Jan had left for town, Bob decided he'd busy himself in the barn while waiting for Monford to pick up the equipment. He was starting out the front door when the telephone started to ring. Walking briskly toward the kitchen, he caught it on the third ring.

"Hello, Bob?" the voice said.

"Dan, is that you?"

"Yeah, it's me."

His immediate thought was that Dan had information concerning Jan's identity. Positive identification meant she would be leaving soon, and he sensed a sudden feeling of loneliness.

"Are you calling in regard to Jan?" Bob asked hesitantly.

"Yeah... got a report back on her fingerprints. It's negative. They couldn't get a match. The woman evidently has never been fingerprinted."

"What about her picture?"

"It's being distributed throughout the northwest newspapers. We'll just have to hope someone recognizes her and comes forward. Bob there is one other thing we can do."

"What's that?"

"Dental records, but that's a long shot, and it could be expensive, since we don't know where she's lived."

"Isn't there some central agency where dental records are kept?"

"Nope, that's why I say it's a long shot. A lot of door knocking on dentist offices would have to be done. I think it would be a waste of time unless we knew precisely where she's from."

Bob drew a deep breath, then exhaled. "If she's never been fingerprinted, we might never find out who she is."

"Well, if AFIS can't match her prints, they'll send them to the FBI for a check. If she has no prints on file there, and doesn't regain her memory, you're absolutely right. I can come to the ranch and explain the situation to her."

"No, you don't have to do that," Bob said. "She and Stephan are in town doing some shopping. I'll tell her myself when she gets back." He was dreading having to do that. He didn't want her to be hurt by the fact they hadn't found anything yet, but he knew she would have to know.

When Jan and Stephan returned from town, Bob took her aside and gently explained to her what the marshall had found out, and he was right. She was hurt and depressed for most of the day. But he kept assuring her that the picture had just been distributed to the papers, and it would probably take some time to hear anything. It seemed to ease her mind some, and by evening her spirits were up.

On Saturday evening, Jan showered and carefully applied her make-up. Thinking of the apparel she would wear, she finally decided on a dress rather than jeans and a western shirt. After she was finished, she examined herself in the full-length mirror and she was pleased at how she looked. She found herself wanting to look nice for Bob rather than Bill, hoping to stir something in him.

During this time, Bob and Stephan had been tending to their stock. Jan sat at the table, aimlessly leafing through a magazine when they came in from the barn. She felt slightly nervous. She rose from her seat and poured Bob a glass of iced tea.

Stephan picked up his comic book, took his usual seat at the table, and started reading.

"Thanks," Bob said. He took the cool glass from her, then sat at the table. He glanced up at her and smiled. Her hair was fixed in a stylish manner, and the make-up she wore accentuated her beauty. She's gorgeous, he thought.

Had Stephan not been in the room he would have expressed his pleasure at how pretty she looked. It had been his intention to take her into town tonight and join in the festivities, but, wanting it to be a surprise for her, he hadn't mentioned it.

She returned to her seat at the table. It seemed an awkward moment for her. She watched Bob, and could see something in his eyes that reflected an appreciation for her appearance. Perhaps even a question on why she was dressed the way she was, but, he said nothing.

For a lack of anything to say, she asked, "Did you get the horses taken care of?" It was a non-consequential question that had no bearing on what was in her mind. Should she tell him she had a date with Bill Holt? Did he even care? She flicked a quick glance at the clock; it was a quarter after seven. Well, he would know soon enough, she thought.

"Yep, we got them all fed and bedded down." He gulped down the iced tea, then stood up. "I think I'll clean up and get this horse smell off of me," he said, starting down the hallway.

Stephan remained at the table, reading his book and paying no attention to either of them. He only looked up when car lights flashed through the living room window.

"That must be Bill," she said, getting up from the table.

"What's he doing here?" Stephan asked, pretending not to know what was going on.

"He asked me to go to a dance this evening and I accepted."

"Oh. Well, have a good time," he said nonchalantly.

Jan opened the door when Bill climbed the porch steps. "Are you ready to go?" he asked.

"Yes, I'm ready," she replied.

After she closed the door behind her, Stephan listened to her high heels clicking on the porch and on down the steps. He returned to reading his book, feeling very pleased with himself, but he felt the impact would have been greater if his father had been in the room when Bill came for her. Again, he had seen the flickering light in his father's eyes when he gazed at how nicely dressed she was.

Bob showered and shampooed his hair. While the luke-warm water rinsed his body, he started thinking of Jan. She had accepted the shelter of his home, and her presence was having an impact on his lifestyle. Much to the better, he had to admit. But, beyond that, he was becoming more and more attracted to her. He let his mind wonder to how she would feel in his arms and the touch of her lips upon his. He shook his head violently. Get those thoughts out of your mind, boy, he told himself. You're not even sure she thinks of you in that way.

He stepped from the shower and dried himself. Standing before the mirror and running a brush through his hair, he looked at his shaggy beard. Maybe she don't like all this face hair. Ain't said nothing about it, though, one way or the other, he thought. Reaching into the vanity drawer, he pulled out his old shaving mug and brush, then set it beside the sink. Looking at the mug for a moment, he thought of his wife. Then he heard himself saying barely above a whisper. "Forgive me, Laura; maybe it's time."

For a moment he felt like he had no control over his movements. He thrust the mug under hot running water and the brush swirled, building a soapy lather. It seemed in an instant his beard contained the thick, creamy foam. He watched his face emerge when the beard fell away under the strokes of the straight razor, a strange moment for him.

A few minutes later, when Bob walked into the dining room, a look of shock registered on Stephan's face. He had never seen his father without his beard; it was like looking at a stranger. His eyes traveled from his clean, shaven face to the neatly-pressed white shirt, blue jeans and decorative western boots Bob was wearing. Stephan also saw him holding a new Stetson hat in his hand.

"You shaved your beard off! Why?"

"It was time, son. Where's Jan?"

"You did it because of her, didn't you?" His voice sounded strained. "And you're all dressed up for her, too, ain't you?"

"I just asked you where Jan was." He was trying to keep his voice unpretentious.

"She's gone."

"What do you mean, gone? Where?" he asked, keeping his voice calm.

"Bill came for her. They went to the dance."

Stephan saw the jowls in his father's face tighten. "Bill Holt? She went to the dance with him?"

"That's what she said."

He faked a chuckle, but his insides were writhing. "Got to hand it to him. He don't miss a beat," Bob said. Then he walked into the kitchen and gazed out the window. It was more to hide the disappointment he felt, but he could feel his son staring at him. After composing himself, he walked into the living room and sat in his favorite tilt-back chair.

Stephan followed after him. "You were going to take her into town, wasn't you, Dad?" he asked, throwing himself on the couch.

Without looking at him, Bob answered, "Well, I thought it would be a nice thing to do. She hasn't been out at all, and it is a holiday. I'm just glad that she's having some fun."

"Then you don't care if she went."

"Of course not," he lied.

"Then how come all of a sudden you shave off your beard?"

"I was just getting tired of it, that's all."

The answer to his question seemed to satisfy Stephan's curiosity. He flipped on the television set and began watching a comedy show.

Bob leaned back and pulled a Western Horseman magazine from the bookrack beside his chair. Ordinarily the book held articles of interest for him, but his concentration was on anything but the articles. His mind was visualizing Jan in the arms of Bill Holt, and he started talking to himself mentally. Why didn't she at least let him know she was going to the dance with Bill? For that matter, why hadn't he said something of what was on his mind? Maybe she would have gone with him instead of Bill. Anyway it was too late now. He leafed through the pages rapidly, then grabbed another copy. Hours had passed and still the images of her flowed through his mind. He envisioned the seductive way she looked. The dress she was wearing was a one-piece, form-fitting outfit that hit just above her knee, and the high-heeled shoes gave her calf and ankle an appealing shape. He knew the feelings he was beginning to develop for her were running deeper, but, with all the problems surrounding her situation, he felt reluctant to announce his feelings.

At first she was just a woman who had had some sort of accident and lost her memory. Now, he knew her as a warm person who had come into his life and touched him. He was aware of the changes he'd made, and the changes in Stephan because of her presence.

He glanced at the clock; it was nine thirty. Knowing he wouldn't be able to sleep, he returned the magazines to the rack. He got out of the chair, he said, "Think I'll go into town and have a couple of beers, Stephan. You better think about getting to bed."

That was not unusual for him to make the trek into town on a Saturday night. He was surprised that Stephan made no comment at his decision.

"No one will recognize you without your beard," Stephan joked, laughing.

"Maybe not. I'll try to fool them," he said, grabbing his Stetson hat and starting for the door.

Within a few minutes, he was in the pickup, heading toward town. While maneuvering the pickup along the winding road, a thought crossed his mind. Maybe she'll think I'm checking up on her. Then again, maybe I won't see her at all. Anyway, if I do run into her and Bill, I just won't pay them no mind.

SIX

Winthrop was buzzing with activity. The tourists, who thirsted for the flare of the old west, flowed into the town. A multitude of people flooded the only two saloons, and the parking spaces along the street were filled. Bill pulled his car into the John Wayne building lot, two blocks from the Palace lounge and restaurant.

When they entered the Palace, they could hear the blaring country-western music filling the room. While, they were pushing their way through the boisterous crowd, a shrill whistle caught Bill's attention. Looking in that direction, he spotted a friend. Once they reached the man, Bill introduced Jan over the noise of the music and the crowd.

"How about helping me and the lady get a table, Harry?"

While Harry's eyes searched the room, Jan noticed that he was only about three inches taller than herself, and his brown hair was cut so short that it gave him a boyish appearance. She didn't feel that he was old enough to even be allowed in a bar, let alone work in one.

"Come on," Harry said, motioning. He spotted a small table for two. After sitting down and getting comfortable, they placed an order for drinks, which Harry promptly returned to them.

An hour passed, and Bill and Jan had danced nearly the whole time, occasionally breaking to sip the iced nectar and cool themselves.

More people crowded into the saloon; getting drinks was taking longer. Bill politely excused himself and pushed his way through the crowd, cornering Harry.

"Hey, buddy, want to do me a favor?" he asked.

"Make it quick. They're running my tail off tonight."

Bill jerked his head in Jan's direction.

"I'll make it worth your while to keep the drinks flowing."

"Got something going there, Bill?" Harry asked, raising his eyebrows, then added, "You lucky SOB. Where in the hell did you find something like her? She's really a gem!"

Bill's lustful eyes glared down at Harry.

"I'll tell you all about her later. Just keep the booze coming and add a little extra to hers, okay?"

"Gotcha covered, guy," Harry said with a smile.

Jan was having a good time, and Bill was jovial and entertaining, but her thoughts kept drifting back to Bob. Closing her eyes, she imagined his strong arms holding her, but that feeling soon vanished and was replaced by irritation that he hadn't asked her to the dance. Didn't he know that she would have jumped at the chance to go with him?

Bill found her attractive, but perhaps Bob didn't, and that thought hurt. She started to think she had misjudged the wanting look she'd noticed in his eyes. Maybe it was simply wishful thinking on her part. Even though she was feeling hurt and rejected, she found herself constantly watching the door, wishing he would suddenly appear.

The evening wore on. She was becoming giddy and lightheaded from the cocktails. When the music stopped, the group leader announced they were taking a break.

"Want to catch a breath of fresh air?" Bill asked, still holding her in his arms.

"Yes, I would," she replied, thinking the fresh air would clear her mind.

The cool evening breeze felt refreshing, but did little to clear her head; she was still woozy from the drinks. She felt his arm slip around her waist, giving her support.

"Let's sit in the car for awhile," she suggested. "Those seats are so hard and uncomfortable, not to mention my poor feet."

When they reached the car, he unlocked the door for her, then walked around and climbed in on his side.

Jan sighed and relaxed comfortably in the soft seat. The alcohol was taking its toll. She thought, if she could just rest for awhile, she would feel better.

"Thank you for bringing me to the dance. It's been fun," she said, her voice slurred.

Bill turned toward her and placed his arm on the back of the seat. "It's been my pleasure, Jan, but it's not over yet."

Feeling heady, she leaned her head on the back of the seat and gazed at him through hazy eyes. "It's not?"

He dropped his arm around her shoulder. "No," he replied, then gently drew her to him, and kissed her hungrily.

Even though woozy, she was taken by surprise with his suddenness. Her first reaction was to repel him, but his embrace tightened, and his mouth pressed harder against her lips. Suddenly she found herself trapped beneath him. Fear struck in her heart. He started to grapple with her dress. She pleaded with him to stop, but he continued to pull at her dress. While writhing beneath his weight, she tried to pull her dress down, but he was too strong. She moved her head from side to side, trying to avoid his kisses, and fighting even harder to push him off of her.

Bob had arrived in town at ten o'clock. Finding no place along the street to park, he drove to the edge of town and parked close to the John Wayne building. The town was really bustling now with activity and he pushed his way up the wooden boardwalk to Three Fingered Jack's. Easing his way up to the bar, Kate Donovan, the bartender, flashed her eyes in his direction. "Be with you in a minute!" she yelled above the crowd noise.

When she approached him, `Well, if Jan's out having a good time, I think I'll have some fun, too,' he thought to himself. "Busy place," he commented.

"Yeah, it's been like this for hours. What's your pleasure?"

"Gimme a schooner," he said, putting some money on the counter.

Kate filled the iced schooner, then returned. "There you go," she said, reaching for the money.

He looked directly into her eyes and grinned. "Has anybody ever told you that you have a terrific set of legs?" She was wearing a low-cut, white blouse with a ruffled front, tight black shorts and dark pantyhose. Her feet were snugly tucked into high heels. She had short blonde hair shaped into a fashionable style.

"Down, boy," she returned, "but thanks for the compliment."

"You're wearing my favorite color, too...tight black."

Then she stopped in mid-stride and turned to face him. "Bob...is that you?" she asked, squinting at him.

"You got it," he replied, grinning broadly.

A smile parted her lips. "My God...you shaved off your beard! No wonder I didn't recognize you."

"Now tell me the truth, Kate. You didn't mind what I said at all, did you?"

"You ought to hear some of the things **these** bozos say. You were being nice. Where have you been the last couple of weeks or so?" she asked in a softer voice.

"Been pretty busy, Kate."

"Yeah, and I have a good notion why."

"Now, Kate, who you been talking to?" he asked, imagining what the local gossips had been saying.

"Hell, Bob, it's all over town about that woman living with you," she sniped.

"Whoa now. There's no woman living with me and that's a fact."

"Then what's she doing there if she isn't living with you?"

"Well, if you've been listening to the right people, then you know why she's there."

"At least you could have come to me and explained the situation yourself," she said through pouting lips, "instead of letting me hear it from everyone else."

Bob was not surprised by what she was saying. Kate and her husband were the first two people he and Laura had met after moving into the area. Eventually, they all had become friends.

Kenneth Charles Donovan, called himself K.C. His initials became his nickname, and those who knew him called him Casey. He and Kate owned a small cattle spread not far from Winthrop. It was a run-down ranch that Casey had spent several years trying to rebuild. Time went on, it had become a financial burden and led to heavy indebtedness, which caused problems in their relationship and ultimately a divorce.

Casey moved from the area, but Kate stayed, taking her present job as a bartender at Three-Fingered Jack's. When Laura became ill and passed away, Bob retained his friendship with her. She had helped him through a difficult period. In time their relationship had taken on a new dimension, however, without intimacy. Bob knew Kate had designs on him, but he never could think of her as anything more than a friend.

Bob was at a loss for words, and the moment was awkward for him. He was about to explain when a voice at the bar shouted, "Hey, we need some service over here!"

"I'm coming!" Kate shouted back. Then, leaning her face close to Bob's, she asked, "Did you leave her at home with Stephan?"

"Nope. She had a date tonight," he replied.

"Oh? Well, it's nice she's getting out," Kate beamed.

"Why don't you stick around till closing?" she suggested in parting.

"Could be I'll just do that," he called after her. He was thankful for the abrupt interruption. While Kate was kept busy at the bar, Bob finished his beer, then mingled with the crowd, his eyes searching for Jan.

Even though he was having fun teasing Kate and kidding around with his friends, his thoughts were consumed with Jan. He kept wondering if she was having a good time with Bill Holt. Secretly, he hoped she was having a miserable time, but then became angry with himself. He knew the harsh thoughts rushing through his mind were only out of jealousy, and he had no right to be. After all, he had no claim on her. The warm looks she would send his way were probably just out of gratitude for being a friend when she needed one.

'Why do relationships have to be so complicated?' he asked himself. Why couldn't he have met some nice, simple woman? No, he has to meet a beautiful, desirable woman with amnesia! But he found himself smiling, thinking of how well she had fit into his life. They had an easy manner with each other. She had done wonders with the house, and he enjoyed coming in after a long day of work, knowing she would be there. He also admired her for not sitting and dwelling on her memory loss. But it seemed odd to him that she wouldn't have a husband searching the country for her. He watched the many couples dancing close together. A vision appeared in his mind of the two of them dancing slowly to the music. He was holding her close, very close. They were one, smiling into each other's eyes. He could smell the scent of the perfume in her hair when they twirled to the music. Suddenly, an overwhelming need flooded him. He decided to go to the Palace to see if he could spot her there. He just had to see her.

When he was about to walk out the door, he ran into Marshall Dan Miller. They tried to side-step each other, but they moved in unison. Dan looked at Bob with surprise in his eyes.

"Bob,...you shaved off your beard!"

"Yeah, how about that? How do I look?" Bob asked, standing back to let him get a better view.

"You look great. I thought you'd never shave that miserable thing off." He laughed.

"What are you doing in here, Dan?"

"Well, with all the people in town tonight, I thought I'd better do a check and see that things weren't getting out of hand."

"Have you found out any more information about Jan?" Bob asked hesitantly.

"No... if I had, I would have called her. I thought you'd have her with you tonight, bein' as there's a big dance and all. Did she stay out at the ranch with Stephan?" the marshall asked with a grin.

"No," Bob replied irritably. He knew the marshall was egging him on and he didn't like it one bit.

"I detect a little testiness in your voice. Where is she?"

Bob answered in a lowered voice. "She had a date."

"What? I didn't hear ya."

"She had a date tonight," Bob said, raising his voice.

"Well, doesn't look like she's lettin' any grass grow under her feet."

Bob shrugged his shoulders. "She's old enough to do what she wants."

"She's gittin' to ya, ain't she? You're probably hopin' she don't remember her past," the marshall suggested.

"Don't be ridiculous! I want her to remember who she is. Besides, I don't see where you're doing all that great a job at finding out any information."

Now it was the marshall's defenses that were in high gear. "Hey, Bob, I've done everything I can. You know her picture's been distributed throughout all the northwest newspapers, and it just takes time. If she'd been fingerprinted at some point, it'd be a lot easier."

Bob knew he'd gone too far. "I'm sorry, Dan, I know your resources are limited. It's just that I know it's on her mind constantly, even though she puts up a good front."

"I wish there was more I could do for the lady, Bob."

"Yeah, me too. Well, I got to get going."

When Bob started to away, the marshall reached out and gripped his arm. "If you see her around tonight, I don't want no trouble, okay?"

Bob met his eyes, touched the brim of his hat and walked away.

Shortly past midnight Bob entered the Palace Saloon. The dance floor was empty. His eyes scanned the tables for Jan and Bill, but, not seeing them, he moved into the lounge. He stood by the entrance looking around the room. They were not there either.

He stepped outside, walked toward the bank, then leaned against the wall. Watching for her, he found himself observing the people milling about, and he began to feel foolish. Suppose he **did** find her, what the hell would he do? Take her away from Bill? That's nonsense, he thought. It was her choice to go out with him. He had no right to chase after her, and that's exactly what he was doing.

He moved from the wall and headed back to Three Fingered Jack's. Kate had wanted him to stay until closing time, but, halfway there, he decided to go back to the ranch. He shouldn't have come to town in the first place.

Walking back to his pickup, he thought he could hear the voice of a woman protesting.

"Get off of me! I mean it!" Bob heard the raised voice again and stopped. He moved closer to the car, then he recognized the auto; it belonged to Bill Holt. He stepped back and peered through the half-closed window. The voice he heard left no doubt in his mind that it was Jan's. Instant anger flooded his senses, as he watched the struggling, writhing figure beneath Bill.

With one swift move he jerked the door open, and his large hand reached inside and grabbed a handful of hair. He heard a surprised cry from within the car when he pulled Bill out and threw him to the ground like a piece of trash. Bill lay on his back, glaring at the man standing over him.

"What the hell do you think your doin', fella?" he shouted angrily. Jumping to his feet, he stepped forward to confront his assailant.

"The lady was objecting. You should show more respect."

"You meddling jerk! I'll show you respect!" he shouted, charging Bob with his fist raised.

Bob sidestepped the charge, and grabbing his arm, he spun him around and had him in a half-nelson move. His lips were close to Bill's ear. "I know who you are, Bill. You want to be held for attempted rape?"

"Who are you and why should you care?" Bill asked, still struggling to get out of the hold.

He turned him loose with a shove. "Bob Malloy, that girl is staying at my ranch. Your date is over."

Bill, making sure it was Bob, looked at him, "You've shaved your beard."

"That's right. Now do you want to go to jail? If you do, I'll be more than glad to bring charges!"

Bill was single, and if charges were brought before him, he wouldn't get anywhere in this town. "I'm sorry, Bob. I had too much to drink. Let's forget the whole thing."

Bob raised one hand with the thumb pointing the direction. "Get going."

Jan was breathing heavily. She was still struggling when the weight was suddenly lifted from her. Her head was spinning, induced by actively resisting Bill. She relaxed a moment to catch her breath, then wobbled to an upright position. She stumbled from the car, and had little control of her legs. The alcohol was working its effects on her equilibrium. Still, she was well aware of what Bill's intentions were, but unsure why she was suddenly spared. Using the car for support, she walked around it, and her blurred vision caught Bill talking to someone.

She leaned against the car while her dulled mind pieced together what had happened. This tall, figure of a man had saved her from being raped.

"Are you all right, Jan?" Bob asked, rushing over to her. His face was lined with concern.

"Yes...yes, I'm all right," she replied with a slurred voice, then leaned unsteadily against the car. She was cognizant, even through her hazy mental condition, that somehow this man knew her, but she had never seen him before. "Thank...you...for helping me." She gazed up at him, then in a semi-slurred voice she said, "You know who I am, but who are you? Do I know you?"

"You should... you've been living at my ranch for the last three weeks."

She laughed sarcastically. "Oh, no, I haven't. I live with a man and his son, and he's got this terrible stringy beard," she said, making a funny face.

"His son has a shaggy beard?" Bob smiled teasingly.

"No..." she shook her head angrily, and waved her arm brushing his words away. "The man has the beard. His son can't even grow peach fuzz...yet."

"I think I'd better get you home," he said, moving toward her.

"I'm not going with you!" she yelled, stumbling away from him. "I don't know who you are, and I'm not about to let you take me anywhere!"

Without a further word, Bob threw her 120-pound body over his shoulder and headed for the pickup.

She pounded her hands against his back and kicked her legs, but he held her securely. He was strong and her weight was nothing to him. When reaching the pickup, he set her down, then fumbled in his pocket for the keys to unlock the door.

She recognized the truck, and in her stupor she wondered what this man was doing with Bob's pickup. She stood studying him while he inserted the key into the lock.

"Bob...Bob Malloy...it's you! I...thought..." she stammered.

"You thought what?" he said with heated sarcasm in his voice.

She leaned against the pickup with her arms folded, the then hung her head, looking at the ground, ashamed. "I don't...know...what I thought."

"Not much wonder. How much have you had to drink?" His tone of voice was still admonishing.

His attitude had a sobering effect, and she looked up sharply to meet the anger she saw in his face. She responded with her own anger. "For your information, I only had three drinks, and besides, it's none of your business. I was having a good time..."

He quickly interjected, "Until I came along and broke it up, eh?"

His implication angered her more. "Oh, so now you think you're some kind of gallant hero. Is that it? Well, I want you to know that I can take care of myself."

His eyes flashed at her. "Are you saying you were enjoying your little tete-a-tete in his car?"

She stood looking up into his wrathful eyes. "If that's what you want to think, go ahead," she mumbled, near tears.

"That's what you're telling me, isn't it? You were enjoying it."

"No...I wasn't, and why are we fighting?"

"I'm not fighting!" he shouted.

"Why are you so mad at me?"

"I'm not mad at you!" he shot back in the same tone.

"Then why are you acting this way?"

He remained silent and looked away from her.

Her voice turned soft. "Well, for what it's worth," she said, "I'm glad you came along when you did. That horrible man had every intention of having his way with me." Slowly he turned his eyes toward her. "Why did you go out with him in the first place, Jan?"

"He asked me to go," she answered. "I didn't know what kind of a person he was. He seemed so friendly."

"Are you in the habit of going out with the first guy that asks you?" he challenged, still angered.

"At first I turned him down. I was waiting for you to ask me."

"Yeah? Well, if you must know, I had every intention of asking you."

"Why didn't you say something sooner?"

"I wanted to surprise you, that's why," he responded, his voice softening.

The bright moonlight was showering a glow of yellow light over them. When she looked up at him, he could see the sparkle of moonbeams reflected in her eyes and the beautiful shine it put to her auburn hair. Seeing her innocence, he felt a rush of desire to take her in his arms, to taste the sweetness of her lips upon his. He moved closer and placed his hand on her bare arm.

His warm hand gently touching her sent a sensuous shiver through her body. She tilted her face toward him and saw desire in his soft eyes. She stood still, waiting, with eyes partially closed, anticipating the touch of his lips upon hers. Instead, he nudged her toward the open door of the pickup. "We better head for home," he whispered and quickly walked to the other side.

Her anticipation of his lips pressing against hers ended in disappointment. What was the matter with him? The mood, the moonlight, all the ingredients for a moment of romance were there, yet he refused to capture that moment. Reluctantly she slid into the passenger seat and slammed the door shut.

"Will Stephan still be up?" she asked.

"Don't think he will be at this hour. Why?"

"I just don't want him to see me...this way."

Bob started the engine and headed out of town.

Jan lay her head on the back of the seat. "I can't believe how foolish I was to go out with that man. He just wanted my body."

"Well, I'll tell you one thing, if that idiot ever shows his face at the ranch again, I'll give him the same treatment he got tonight and then some!"

She sat huddled on her side of the truck just watching him. Though disappointed at his elusiveness to kiss her, she smiled, feeling a warming sensation surround her over his protectiveness, and it was then she realized that he really did care for her.

The sun was just rising on a clear October morning when Jan awoke to prepare breakfast for Stephan before he left for school. When Stephan walked into the kitchen, she greeted him cheerfully, then set his breakfast on the table.

"Thank you," he said with a forced smile on his face.

Stephan knew nothing of the events that had taken place the night of the dance, and he wondered why Bill had not called or come to the ranch to see her. Nothing had seemed to change between Jan and his father, except they were growing closer and closer. His plan hadn't worked, and his fears and confusion had returned. He didn't want to feel this way, but he couldn't seem to help himself. This woman had come in and completely taken over their home. A home he once had shared only with his father. He felt that the strong bond between them was now lessening with each passing day, and it hurt him deeply.

The fall season moved on, Jan found herself becoming more interested in the activities of the ranch. She learned from Bob that he had joined in a contract through a local cattle broker to winter-feed 500 head of yearling calves. On the day Bob was to go into town to sign the necessary papers, she went along, intending to do some shopping. When he pulled the pickup in front of the cattle broker's office, he said, "If there's anything you ever want to know about horses, Lawrence Manning is the man to ask."

Bob explained that Lawrence, who was nearing seventy, had raised horses for years. His interest didn't lie in the running horse, but more toward the show horse. He had produced some of the finest show horses in the country and had several Grand Champion and Reserve Championship awards to his credit. Although horses were his first love, cattle became more lucrative, and, at his age, it required less time and much less travel. His office was adorned with photographs and trophies of those past triumphs.

"I don't know enough about a horse to ask any questions," Jan replied.

"Some day you might," Bob noted, smiling.

"Oh, are you going to teach me?" she quipped.

"Well, now that all depends... because I think you're afraid of horses," he said with a baiting look on his face.

"I never **said** I was afraid," she miffed indignantly.

"You wouldn't sit on Blue! Remember?"

"Oh, so that means I'm afraid, huh?"

He looked at her; her words were offering him a challenge. "You ever ridden?"

"I don't know. I can't remember. Remember?" She laughed. Jan was enjoying the bantering. She had found that he did have a jovial sense of humor about him. In fact, she was finding that he exhibited a lot of fine qualities. He had come to her rescue on two occasions, and when he was near, she didn't feel alone; the frustration of her amnesia even seemed lessened.

"Maybe we can do something about that," he said, opening the pickup door, startling her out of her thoughts.

"Want to come in with me?"

"Sure, why not," she said, wanting to meet this man who commanded so much of Bob's respect.

Later that week, Saturday morning, Jan's attention to her household chores was disrupted by the sound of bawling cattle, and she stepped outside onto the porch to watch the cattle stringing by the house and into the open fields.

The ranch encompassed 400 acres that stretched nearly a mile in length from the house. The rich soil was still producing growth that would sustain two head of cattle per acre over the next few weeks. The sight of the drovers and the sound of their short, ear-piercing whistles, hazing the cattle along, presented a moment in the romantic flare of the old west.

Jan suddenly felt she had been thrown into the past. Puzzled by this feeling, her mind grasped and clung to it. Something in her lost memory was trying to surface. It was then that an image appeared in her mind of a young child sitting alone in a large room. She presumed it to be herself. The walls in the room were shelved and lined with books. She was sitting in an over-stuffed chair, reading a book that was almost too large for her to hold.

The image of the room was so vivid, but where was it? What significance did it hold for her? She concluded that the feeling she had experienced with the sight of the cattle only could have been in relation to something she had read when she was a little girl. Closing her eyes and concentrating hard, she searched with her mind's eye, hoping it might be a key to opening her memory, but it remained just a room filled with books. The moment was so disturbing she quickly returned to her household duties in an effort to dispel these thoughts.

That night, in the silence of her darkened room, sleep did not come easily for her. Her developing feelings for this man who had found her were growing deeper. She started to think of her situation, analyzing just where she fit into the scheme of things. The remembrances she'd been experiencing weren't enough to piece together a whole lifetime. They only confused her more because they were so erratic and infrequent.

She concluded there was not much she could do unless she regained her memory totally, or someone came forth who knew her.

Not knowing what her life had been or what it entailed, she tried to keep her feelings toward Bob in check. However, that was easier said than done. He was like a magnet, drawing on her emotions, and she couldn't help the growing passion she felt for him. When she looked at him, she saw a virile man with attractive features who weakened her defenses.

She remembered the night of the dance and how he had come to her aid. She also remembered how much she had wanted him to kiss her. The desire was evident in his face, but he wouldn't respond to it. 'Why?' she asked herself. It had to be because of Stephan. She knew that he loved his son very much, and would not do anything intentionally to hurt him.

Sleep eventually came to her, and when she awoke the following morning a new attitude filled her mind. It was a new day, and with it, came a new thought. It truly would be the first day of the rest of her life. Knowing who she was and what her life had been ,was no less important to her, but she no longer could let it be ever present on her mind. She could not remain stagnant, waiting for the marshall to call with news of her past or the prospect of someone suddenly appearing on the doorstep claiming to know her.

SEVEN

Jan rolled out of bed and prepared to meet the day. When she walked into the kitchen, after pouring herself a cup of the brew, she walked to the table and sat down next to him. "Is Stephan up yet?" she asked, gazing at his clean-shaven face.

Bob was sitting at the table having coffee and reading his Western Horseman magazine. "No, he's still in bed," Bob answered, putting his magazine aside. Their eyes met and held momentarily.

"Have I mentioned that you look much better without your beard?"

"No," he teased. "I didn't think you noticed. I shaved it off a long time ago."

"How could I help not noticing?" She laughed.

"It's taken you enough time to say something," he said, a slight smile crossing his lips.

"Why did you shave it off?" She wondered if she was the reason, but wanted to hear him admit it.

A flush crossed his face. "No particular reason... it was just time," he said, getting up to refill his cup.

When he returned to the table, they sat awkwardly silent. Finally Jan spoke. "I think we should have a talk."

"About what?" he asked, noticing the intense look on her face. "About the whole situation concerning me. I've been here for eight or nine weeks now."

"So? I have no complaints." An anxiety started to fill him over the direction this conversation was taking.

"But I can't continue to stay here forever. It isn't fair to you or to me."

"Like I said, I have no complaints. Besides, where would you go that's any better than right here?"

"I don't know, but I feel I'm a burden. I'm an extra mouth to feed."

Bob felt a twinge in his stomach. If he were faced with her situation, that's exactly how he would feel. Had she made that kind of decision within the first few days of him finding her, he wouldn't have cared less. But with her continued presence, he realized how lonely he'd become after Laura's death. Sure, he had Stephan and he loved his boy more than life itself, but it wasn't the same as the companionship and love of a woman. Somehow, he had to convince her to stay. He looked directly into her eyes.

"Get that notion out of your mind. How can you say you're a burden? You take care of the house, and do a damn good job. Plus, your presence here has been a good influence on Stephan. No, Jan, you're no burden, you're an asset."

"You must consider Stephan. He hasn't come right out and said anything, but we both know that he would like to see me go."

"You forget about Stephan," he said in a raised voice.

Jan put her finger to her lips, cautioning him to lower his voice.

"Well, I'm sorry, but I'm the head of this house and he has to learn that there are other people's feelings to consider. Since his mother died, I've tried to be patient with him, but I can't live my life entirely for him," he added harshly.

She was surprised by his statement. She wanted to test the water with him. She had to know if he had any affection for her, or if what she had been sensing was only her imagination. His last statement told her that maybe Stephan wasn't the reason he'd been holding back. "I agree, but that has nothing to do with my situation..." she finally said.

"It has everything to do with you, Jan." His response to her statement was words only in his mind. He didn't intend to suddenly blurt them out, and it was unexpected to him.

Bob's gaze dropped to her full lips. He could feel the heat creeping from his neck to his face. He shifted his eyes, looking blankly at the table.

She instinctively knew that this was the time to push even further. "What do you mean, it has everything to do with me?" she asked, looking directly at him.

Why is she probing me with these questions? Bob asked himself. He flicked his eyes at her. "Well...ah...I just meant that...I feel responsible for you, that's all," he sputtered.

"Why should you feel responsible for me? I'm an adult and fully capable of taking responsibility for myself. I appreciate all that you have done for me, but, if I want to leave you should respect that," she continued badgering.

"Dammit, Jan, I don't want you to leave," he said sternly, rising from his chair.

"Why don't you want me to go?" she asked, getting up to stand next to him.

"Hell...because...winter's coming soon..." he stammered.

"That's no reason to stay," she said, her eyes burning into his.

"Because...because ...I'll miss you," he finally confessed, but his voice was barely above a whisper.

"What was that? I couldn't hear you."

"Dammit, I'll miss you!" he shouted.

"Then why didn't you say that in the first place! I'd miss you and Stephan, too, if I were to leave."

"Does this mean you're not leaving?" he asked hopefully.

"I'm not sure. I need more time to think about it."

Bob couldn't grasp what was going through her mind. She had pulled words from him that he hadn't intended to say.

"I'll make a deal with you."

"What kind of deal?" she asked.

"Well, you agree to stay until we race Blue. If nothing confirms your identity, and you still have your memory loss, you can leave. I won't stand in your way."

"When is the race?"

"It's in May."

She counted on her fingers. "That's about seven months away."

"Yep, that's right. Is it a deal?"

She had no real intention of leaving, and only had used the idea as a vehicle to learn his feelings toward her. But she was disappointed by his proposal, and hoped it didn't show in her expression. He only said he'd miss her. Had she misread the signals from him? Deep inside, her intuition was telling her to give him more time.

"Okay, it's a deal," she said, putting her hand out to him.

He reached out and took her small hand within his to bind the agreement. They stood for a moment, still grasping hands. The awareness between them was electrifying. Jan felt the fire of his touch throughout her whole body. Somewhere an inner voice told her that no man in her past ever could have caused the pounding in her chest that was happening now.

Sensuous feelings flowed through his body from the touch of her hand in his. He looked deeply into her alluring eyes. Could she possess the same feelings? The yearning to taste the sweetness of her lips was like a driving force. Suddenly he found himself bending his head toward her lips, but the magic of the moment was broken by the clicking of Stephan's boots moving down the hallway.

Their hands parted quickly. "I suppose I should start getting breakfast," she said, feeling shattered that Stephan had chosen this precise moment to come into the room.

Bob slumped into his chair. That heated moment had been broken, for, had he kissed her just once, he knew he would not have been able to stop.

"When are you going to teach me how to ride a horse?" she asked, nervously setting a skillet on the stove.

Stephan shot a quick look at his father.

"Whenever you're ready," he replied, smiling.

At hearing that his father was going to teach Jan to ride, an anger started to build inside of him. "I think I'll skip breakfast this morning," he announced. He hurriedly reached for his hat, "I have a lot of chores to do."

"Hey, there's no rush, son. Come on and have your breakfast," Bob insisted. "Jan will have it ready in just a minute. You can wait."

The tone of Bob's voice stopped Stephan just when he was about to open the door. "Okay," he said, reluctantly taking a seat at the table.

Jan sensed the hostility in Stephan, but ignored it. "Are your horses gentle?"

"Sure. I have one that's never been ridden before. I figure you can both learn together," he responded with a teasing smile.

Stephan laughed, while picturing her in his mind getting bucked off of a horse.

She threw a glance at the two of them. "Are you serious?" she asked, then saw the smile on his face.

"Of course not. I wouldn't want to take a chance on getting the horse hurt."

"Oh you, thanks for the consideration."

They all three laughed over their bantering.

When breakfast was over, she watched Bob and Stephan leave the house to do their chores. She had seen the look of hostility in Stephan's eyes when she had asked about learning to ride, and knew that was why he had made an excuse not to eat breakfast. Well, she was going to learn to ride **with** or **without** his approval.

Buck was a gelding; it was the horse Bob was riding the day he'd found her. He was a beautiful chestnut color with white stocking feet. She watched Bob put a rope halter on him then him lead from the stall into the large open barn.

With the headstall in place and the saddle cinched, he felt her body tremble while hoisting her into the saddle.

"Don't be frightened of him. He's gentle," he assured her while he adjusted the stirrups. "Now sit up straight and tell me when you can see the toe of your boot just over your knee."

Jan squirmed around in the saddle a bit, then said, "There, I think that's it."

With the stirrups adjusted, he placed the reins properly in her hands. "When you want to go left, just lay the reins on his neck, like so," he said, demonstrating what he wanted her to do. "You do the same thing when you want to go right. When you want to stop, just pull back gently on the reins. He's well-trained, so keep your hand in front of the saddle horn and only use your wrist to move the reins. You got it now?"

"I think so," she answered tensely.

"Okay. He's all yours."

She sat up straight, expecting the horse to move, but Buck remained stationary. "Giddyup," she finally said. "Come on, Buck, giddyup!"

Bob looked up at her, pushed his hat back on his head, and laughed at her child-like expression.

"What's so funny?" she asked, looking at him with her eyebrows knitted together.

"I didn't teach him **giddyup!** Just nudge him in the flanks with your heels," he said, continuing to chuckle.

At the touch of her heels, Buck moved forward at a brisk walk. When she tugged at the reins, he stopped. Nudging him with her heels once more, he began to move. She relaxed her hand and Buck moved into a trot. Bob watched her sexy behind bounce in the saddle while Buck circled the large open area. When she stopped the horse, Bob walked toward them.

"Oh, God, I don't think I can take much more of this," she moaned.

"It's all in learning how, Jan. You have to learn to ride by balance. A trot is rough. Just raise yourself out of the saddle when he breaks a trot and try to adjust to his movement. Take him around again," Bob ordered.

She nudged Buck once more. He moved into a trot. She balanced herself on the balls of her feet, putting more of her weight in the stirrups. She circled the open area of the barn twice, then stopped where Bob was waiting.

"That's much better," he praised.

Jan dismounted. "This is more work than I thought," she said, rubbing the sore muscles in her legs.

"You're not used to it, that's all. You're using muscles in a different way."

"Yeah, some I didn't know I had!" She laughed.

"Look, I'll show you something," he said, vaulting into the saddle.

Buck made the large circle. Bob was moving in an entirely different manner. She likened it to a man sitting in a rocking chair.

"How did you make him do that?" she asked when he stopped at her side.

"That's called a canter. You try it," he said, stepping down and handing the reins to her.

Her method of mounting the horse was awkward, but he let her struggle for a moment. "Here, let me show you something," he said, taking the reins and helping her back down.

"See how that stirrup is twisted?"

"Yes," she answered with an increased interest in what he was explaining to her.

"There's a reason for that. It lays facing away from his side. Now watch me," he instructed. With the reins in his left hand, he grasped the saddle horn while facing the rear of the horse. Then he slipped his left foot into the twisted stirrup, springing upward, and at the same time pulling with his left hand on the saddle horn and straightening his leg. It seemed effortless and he moved into the saddle. He explained each of his movements while he performed them. "Now you try it."

It was awkward at first, but, she practiced the move a few times, and her coordination improved.

"I think you have it, Jan," Bob said with a wide grin on his face. "It just takes a little doin' to get the hang of it. Now, hold back on the reins a little, but not too much." Bob instructed. "That's it. Now use your heels."

Buck took two steps, then started the short lope. Instinctively she grabbed the saddle horn, then stood in the stirrups. Concentrating on matching Buck's motion, she eased herself into the saddle. She was surprised at the ease of the ride. Making another two rounds of the area, she brought the horse back to Bob. "Now **that** was fun. I really enjoyed that ride," she said, smiling broadly.

"You looked good up on that old boy, too," he said, complimenting her.

"Thank you, kind sir. But I think I've had enough for today," she replied, rubbing her posterior.

Bob chuckled, watching her rub her backside. "You'll have strawberries on your cheeks, but you'll toughen in," he advised, pulling the saddle off of Buck and replacing it with another.

"Why are you changing saddles?" she asked, puzzled.

"I'm going to check the fences. I want to be sure there's no wire down."

"Oh, thank goodness. I thought you were going to make me ride some more."

"Nope, not today. When you get back to the house, send Stephan out. He can go with me."

Jan gave Stephan the message, then watched through the living room window while the two of them rode into the fields. She felt a flush come over her, and thought of the time she had just spent with Bob. He had been so patient in teaching her to ride, and she especially enjoyed the gentle way he handled her body while helping her in and out of the saddle. She found that she had not thought of her amnesia all day.

Going to the bookcase, she scanned the titles. Finding one of interest, she settled herself comfortably and began to read. The book told of the origin of the Quarter Horse, referring to its beginning, the short horse. The more she read, the more fascinated she became with its history, and rapidly she devoured the pages.

The time was passing quickly for her, and life had settled into certain patterns. The weather was getting colder and the grass no longer grew. They had been feeding cattle since the third week in October, and while Stephan was in school, she helped Bob with the feeding operation. She drove the tractor through the bawling heard while he broke bales of hay and distributed it among them. After completing that chore, they would return to the barn with the tractor and wagon and reload it for the next day.

The work was hard for her in the beginning, but she soon got acclimated to it. She enjoyed sharing the work load with Bob, but she sensed that he was putting up barriers. Although she could see the familiar gaze in his eyes, he had become somewhat distant again. Oh, he wasn't being irritable, like he was the first few days she was there, and she didn't feel like a guest in his home any more, but there was something else happening. She had noticed the lines of tension that creased his rugged face, and there were bags under his pale blue eyes; he hadn't been getting enough sleep. Something was bothering him, and she wondered if Stephan was connected somehow.

It was getting close to Christmas and snow blanketed the ground. Jan's confidence in her ability to ride was increasing. She continued riding every day, but, because of the snow, rode in the large open area of the barn. Sometimes Bob would saddle up Blue and ride along with her.

"When are you going to let me ride Blue?" she asked on one of these occasions.

Bob chuckled. "He's a lot different than, Buck. No...I'm afraid he's too much horse."

"He seems calm enough when you ride him," she replied.

"Well, I've worked him quite a bit. Besides, he's a stud."

"Does that really make a difference?"

"It does to him," he grinned.

Jan understood his meaning and poked at his arm. "Come on, let me try."

"No way, Jan, he's not as well trained as Buck," he warned, stepping off of Blue, then removing the saddle.

"You're not going to let me ride him, are you?"

"Nope, not today...maybe sometime, but much later."

In the evenings Jan continued her self-study of horses, asking questions of Bob concerning things she didn't understand. Her new-found interest, coupled with the daily activities of the ranch, helped to relieve the pressure of her personal situation. The loss of memory and who she really was receded further into the back of her mind. There were times that she was completely free of those thoughts and consciously had to remind herself that she was only here temporarily. But even that didn't concern her any more. She felt certain there was no one special in her life to return to. If there were, they surely would have found her by now. All she cared about now was Bob and Stephan.

Stephan would sit and listen to their conversations, sometimes contributing, but, time went on, and his frustration grew. He could see his father's growing interest in her. It was becoming more obvious to him, and eventually he withdrew from them, feeling completely left out while they became more engrossed with each other.

By keeping house and helping his father with the daily chores, she was slowly replacing his mother. She had been with them so long now that he felt she didn't want to leave. She was even pretending to be interested in horses.

There was nothing he could do to make her want to leave short of being outright nasty to her, and he knew his father would not tolerate that kind of behavior. His plans for her and Bill Holt seemed to have fizzled, and he wondered why. These thoughts filtered through his mind, knowing he would just have to wait for something to happen, but what?

After Stephan left for school and they had completed their morning chores, Bob and Jan headed for town to pick up some supplies.

"I thought we might do some Christmas shopping while we're in town," Bob said.

"You'll have to do the Christmas bit, I don't have any money, remember?"

He glanced at her and their eyes met for a moment. "Look, Jan, you've done more than I could possibly pay you for, and I want you to have a good Christmas, so just charge it to my account."

"Oh, Bob, I can't do that," she protested.

"Sure you can...I insist. This is going to be the best Christmas since..."

She knew what he intended to say but couldn't finish. She saw the flicker of enthusiasm in his eyes of the coming season and didn't want to spoil it.

"All right, if you insist, but you must promise not to pry."

"I promise," he said, grinning.

When they entered the store, Molly was busy ringing up a customer and didn't see Jan and Bob. Jan diplomatically directed Bob to another section of the store. Taking the hint, he browsed while she shopped. Purchasing several items for him and Stephan, she took them to the counter. Molly was just finishing up with a customer when she saw Jan and greeted her in her usual good-natured way.

"Can I have these things gift wrapped, Molly?"

"Sure. We'd be glad to do that, dear."

"If you could put them aside, I'd appreciate it. I don't want Bob to see them. We have some other shopping to do, so I'll pick them up before we head back. He said to charge them to his account."

"Of course. I'll have one of the girls wrap them for you. I don't suppose you've heard anything yet?" Molly asked, placing the items behind the counter.

"No...I'm still waiting."

"It must be a terrible strain on you, dear."

"Surprisingly, it's not all that bad, Molly. Bob's teaching me to ride, and helping him with the chores keeps me pretty busy. But still I'm just taking it a day at a time," she added. She glanced around the store for Bob. Jan turned and saw him talking to a very attractive woman. The woman was eyeing her with an appraising look.

Bob brought the lady over to where Jan was standing, "I'd like you to meet, Kate. Kate, Jan," he said, making the introductions.

Kate's eyes bore into Jan's. Her lips parted into a smile, but her eyes held a hint of hostility. "I'm pleased to meet you, Jan," Kate acknowledged, extending her hand. Jan grasped her hand in return; it was cold and unfeeling.

Bob interrupted the tense moment. "I'll let you two women get acquainted while I go pick up some wire. I'll be back in a few minutes, Jan."

The two women moved from the counter so Molly could wait on her other customers. "I understand you're in an unusual situation. I hope you hear something soon," Kate said.

Even though she continued to smile, Jan detected an unsociable attitude in Kate, and she had a feeling she was treading on forbidden territory. I'll bet you would, she thought. "I hope so too," Jan replied sweetly. "Bob has been very good to me. I have a great deal of respect for him. Have you known him long?"

"Long enough. And...we've had our moments," Kate said, raising an eyebrow.

Jan felt the sting of her statement. Did she mean that she had had an intimate relationship, or was she just attempting to let her think they had? She decided it was the latter, for he had not left the ranch in weeks. If he were having an affair with her, there had been no evidence of it since her arrival. Her good sense told her she was implying something that didn't exist between them and immediately took the offensive. "Yes, I know. He's quite a man," Jan returned slyly, thinking two can play **that** game.

Kate's smile evaporated instantly. "You mean he..." She didn't get to finish her question. They both became aware that Bob had come back into the store. He announced that he had the wire loaded and was ready to go.

"It's been so nice talking to you, Kate. You must come out and visit us sometime," Jan said with a sharp tone.

"Yes, you can count on it," Kate replied, looking sternly into her eyes. Flashing a glance at Bob, the pleasant smile returned to her face. "Now don't be such a stranger, Bob. You come and visit me."

"I'll do that, Kate," he said, glancing at her when she walked away. Quickly he turned his attention to Jan. "Have you got your things ready to go?"

"We'll pick them up after we do our grocery shopping," she replied stiffly.

Jan sat quietly. Bob pointed the pickup toward home. Her mind was occupied with Kate's insinuation of having a meaningful relationship with him. Her statement had brought forth a feeling of smoldering jealousy within her. The thought of him having slept with Kate bothered her. She was trying to rationalize her thoughts to why it should. She knew she had no right to feel this way.

She had no real claim on him. His wife had been dead for three years, and a man needed the companionship of a woman. It was just a natural thing.

She was beginning to sense that she never had experienced a fulfilling relationship with a man. She glanced at Bob out of the corner of her eye. She was developing so much respect and admiration for him, not to mention the way he made her feel whenever he touched her. Was she falling in love with this sensitive and caring man? Is this what true love was really like?

She was aroused from her thoughts at the sound of his voice. "You're awfully quiet, Jan. Give you a dollar for your thoughts."

"They may not be worth a dollar," she replied.

"Okay, then a penny. That's the usual going rate." He smiled.

"I was thinking of Stephan," she fibbed. "There's times when I feel we're getting closer. Then his attitude changes and he becomes distant. I get the impression he's teetering on the brink between accepting or not accepting me as his friend."

"Yes, I've noticed it, too. I know what he's doing and I'm not happy with it."

Jan wanted to know more of his relationship with Kate, and this was the perfect opportunity to open the door on that subject.

"Kate's a very attractive woman. I understand you've known her for quite some time."

"Yeah, several years, I guess. Laura and I were good friends with Kate and her husband."

"She's married!" she asked in surprise.

"Was married. They're divorced now," he replied.

"Oh, I'm sorry. She seems to show a great deal of interest in you."

Bob shot her a quick glance, then shrugged his shoulders. "Kate's a nice woman, and I admit I like her a lot, but only as a friend. We've helped each other through some difficult times."

She stared into his eyes and felt he was speaking the truth. Soon the jealously she was feeling melted away, and she smiled subtly, inwardly.

EIGHT

It was the Saturday before Christmas and Stephan was excited. This was the day he and his father would scout out a Christmas tree. It was a ritual he had relied on since he was four years old. They rose earlier than usual to feed the cattle, then ate a hearty breakfast before heading out.

Jan prepared a lunch and filled two large thermoses, one containing coffee and the other hot chocolate for Stephan.

"Now bundle up good, Stephan. I don't want you coming down with a cold over Christmas," she said.

"I got plenty of clothes on. I'll stay warm," he snapped.

"Where's your scarf?"

"In my pocket."

"And your gloves?"

"With my jacket," he replied impatiently. It reminded him of his mother fussing over him. He knew he was about to be corrected by his father for his attitude, but caught the glance Jan had flashed him. Pretending he didn't see it, he said, "You ready to go, Dad?"

"Yep, let's saddle up the horses," Bob answered, opening the door.

When they rode past the house, Stephan saw his father wave at Jan, who was watching from the window. With a sudden feeling of remorse for the way he had responded to her earlier, he spun his horse around and waved at her, too.

When Jan saw Stephan wave, it created a strange warm feeling within her. Perhaps it was a beginning, she thought. Maybe she was finally winning him over, a little. All she wanted was for him to accept her like a friend.

She started to think that perhaps God, in His infinite wisdom, had placed her here for a purpose. Was it to fill a vacancy left by the death of Bob's wife, Stephan's mother, or was it for her?

She recalled an earlier feeling. An intuitive feeling of never belonging to anyone. A person among people, set adrift to wonder aimlessly through life without meaningful ties. And, while this thought passed through her mind, she felt an unbearable loneliness encompass her. Why, now, should this perception be so strong within her? Had this possibly been her life in the past? A past she could not remember. A sudden chilling sensation flowed through her body at this thought. If this were truly what her life had been, she wanted no part of it.

Almost five months had passed since she came to the ranch, and now she found she wanted to remain with Bob and his son, regardless of what her past may hold. In these recent months, the three of them had lived like a family, and though she tried to keep her situation in perspective, she was failing. In spite of all her rationalization, she had fallen in love with Bob Malloy.

She no longer could pay heed to the inner voice that cautioned her to beware of her feelings for him. It grew weaker with each passing day. The way in which he looked at her, the stolen glances, and when he touched her, a mysterious warmth raced through her body, and she felt she belonged.

He had to feel these same sensuous feelings. She could see it in his eyes. Could he not sense her feelings for him? Was he so blinded that he could not see himself in her eyes? When a moment of closeness presented itself between them, he would pull back. The fervor she saw in his eyes would suddenly fade, some inner force was shielding him, and she wondered why. Was it truly because of Stephan's emotional tie to his deceased mother, or was it herself? Was he being cautious because he knew nothing of her past?

The ground was covered with four inches of fresh, undisturbed snow. Bob and Stephan crossed the meadowland. With each step of the horses, white powder burst dust, spraying upward to be whiffed away by a slight breeze. Dark clouds hung overhead; the smell of more snow was in the air, and the temperature was dropping.

Two hours from the ranch found them wondering through heavy timber. They entered a small draw, letting the horses pick their way down the slope onto a flat. Dismounting, they tied the horses and set out on foot to inspect the trees. Stephan ran ahead of his father. He had spotted an eight-foot sugar pine.

"Hey, Dad!" he shouted. "Over here. Come look at this one!"

Bob slung the ax over his shoulder and made his way forward. "You think this one will do, eh?" he asked while looking it over.

"Yeah. Look how bushy it is. I think Jan will like it, too, don't you?" Stephan asked enthusiastically.

Stephan's thought of Jan surprised him. It was the first time he had given her consideration in **any** form. Although he was pleased by Stephan thinking of her, he also felt a cautiousness in how he should respond to this seemingly new attitude. "I suppose so," he said, walking around the tree and inspecting it. "We can look at some others, though."

"But I like this one, Dad, let's take it."

"Okay, son. Why don't you scare up some firewood while I cut the tree, and then we'll have some lunch."

Stephan knocked the snow off of the small branches that had fallen from the larger pine trees. Gathering two armfuls and dumping them in a pile, he scraped his boot along the ground, making a bare spot to start a fire. Breaking the smallest of the twigs from the branches, he formed a small mound, then hunkered down to light it. The flames licked at the small twigs, flaring when they hit pockets of sap. Little by little he added larger pieces to the fire, and soon it was producing sufficient heat to warm them.

Bob dragged a log close to the fire that they could sit on, then took the lunch that Jan had prepared from the saddlebags. She hadn't made cold sandwiches, but instead packed hot dogs and buns, so they could have a warm meal. She included squeeze bottles of mustard and ketchup, along with chips and a dessert.

Bob withdrew his hunting knife and cut two branches for cooking the hot dogs.

"Why didn't she just fix us sandwiches like Mom used to do?" Stephan asked.

"Well, son, different people do different things. I expect she wanted us to have a hot lunch. But, if you don't want your share of hot dogs, I'll eat 'em," Bob teased. "Heck with that noise, Dad. I'm **hungry**."

They speared a hot dog on each of their sticks and held them to the fire. "I think she's done a good job of taking care of us, boy," Bob went on.

"Yeah, she's okay...I guess," Stephan said softly. He was thinking back over the months that she'd been with them, remembering the animosity he'd felt toward her in the beginning. She would not tolerate the lifestyle they had become accustomed to. It had angered him that she took over the house in the manner she did. To have voiced that anger would have been disrespectful of her, though he'd wanted to many times. He knew his father had been lenient with him in many things, but disrespect to his elders, he would not abide by. And so, reluctantly, he accepted the changes she'd made.

Time went on, and admiration for her had developed within him that he could not suppress from his mind. Outwardly, though, he refused her offer of friendship. He didn't dislike her, and the pretense to the contrary was becoming more difficult. He saw things pass between Jan and his father, not in words, but in certain actions. And, though his feelings were changing toward her, a fear still haunted his heart. A fear that his father would marry her and forget his mother, forcing him to accept her in his mother's place. "Dad, can I ask you a real important question?"

"Got something on your mind, son?"

"Do you like Jan?"

"Well, of course I do. Don't you?"

"Yeah, I guess so. But I mean, do you really like her, like a girlfriend?"

Bob looked at him, not knowing quite how to respond to the question. He picked up a stick and poked at the fire, then repositioned the hot dog to the flames. "Well, I've never thought of her that way. Jan has been a good friend to both of us, and I think we should respect her for that."

"Yeah, and she's good at helpin' me with English. For someone who lost their memory, how can she do that?" Stephan asked thoughtfully, then added, "Dad, how long is she going to stay with us?"

"The answer to your fist question, I don't know, the mind is a strange thing. The second question, well, her and I made a deal that she would stay until we race Old Blue. Then, if she wanted to, she could leave, unless she gets her memory back, or someone shows up who knows her."

"Suppose she don't and no one comes for her, where's she gonna go?"

"I don't know, son, and I don't think she does either. The way she was dressed when I found her, leads me to believe she must have come from a big city, Seattle maybe. Anyway, the marshall can't seem to find out any information about her."

"What about her picture? They ought to put it in all the papers. I bet someone would see it and come for her."

"That's already been done, Stephan, and nobody's showed up yet. I don't know, maybe she's not even from around this part of the country. Maybe she's from back east, or anywhere in between." "What if, after the race, she decides she wants to stay here?"

"Would you want her to?" Bob asked, hoping for a positive answer.

"Gosh, no, Dad! It's been just you and me since Mom died. We don't need no woman hangin' around all the time."

Bob didn't get the answer he'd hoped for. It would have made it easier had Stephan said yes. But Stephan was just one of the many barriers that had to be overcome. There were others. He started going over things in his mind, like he'd been doing for months now. Who was she? Was there a husband and family frantically searching for her? He couldn't even begin to imagine what they were going through. All he knew was that he desired her more and more each day, and didn't know how long he would be able to keep from telling her how he truly felt about her. He'd seen the yearning look in her eyes and wondered if it were for him, or was it some hidden desire for the husband she was not yet consciously aware of?

He sat looking into the fire. Absently sipping his coffee, he wondered what she was doing at this moment. He found that, whenever doing his chores, his mind was filled with thoughts of her. He would rush through them just to be near her again. Whether she was wearing a dress or a pair of blue jeans and old boots, her loveliness was always present. The warmth he would see in her bright green eyes would cause his heart to melt. Her intelligence was brought forth by the many nights she would spend helping Stephan with his homework. He could see the excitement in her glowing face when he would finally understand what she was explaining to him. Why couldn't Stephan see that she could only be an asset to his life? Why was he being so stubborn about everything? In all the months she'd been with them, she had never lost her temper with him, even though she had good reason. Today, he saw a change in him for the first time. Perhaps he was warming to her, he hoped.

He knew the day would come when she would regain her memory. He felt it deep within himself, and knew that day would bring with it decisions for both of them. He had fallen deeply in love with her, and not knowing what circumstances surrounded her life in the past now became the most devastating obstacle he faced. And he still couldn't seem to get past the idea that he just wasn't worthy of her, even though she'd never once acted that way.

"Maybe you're right, son," he finally said. "But she **is** here, so let's make it the most pleasant Christmas for her that we can. You know she's been pretty good to both of us."

"Yeah, I guess she has. Maybe she'll get the best Christmas present of all," Stephan said.

"What do you mean?"

"Maybe she'll get her memory back, or maybe the marshall will find somebody who knows her."

Bob made no comment on Stephan's statement. The likelihood of that happening so near to Christmas was remote.

It started to snow lightly and the wind had picked up. He drained the last bit of coffee into his cup and recapped the thermos. "We better be heading back. This weather could get nasty," he warned.

Bob repacked the unused food in the saddlebags while Stephan scattered the fire into the snow with his boot, then scraped snow on top of the hot coals, making sure the fire was out. Bob tied his lariat to the trunk of the tree, and they headed for the ranch.

Nearing dusk now and snowing heavily, Jan sat by the window, watching intently for their return. Then, through the thick downpour of snowflakes, she saw them coming up the driveway to the house. Draping her coat over her shoulders, she stepped out onto the porch to greet them.

"You two had me worried. You were gone so long, I thought something had happened to you," she said.

Bob smiled at her. "We'd have been back sooner, but Stephan wouldn't give up until he found a tree that was just right for you."

"That ain't so at all, Jan," Stephan said, getting off his horse. "I found it right off. Dad's just joshin' you."

Bob brought the tree up on the porch and thumped the trunk on the wooden floor, removing the snow it had collected.

"Do you like it? Ain't it got a nice shape?" Stephan asked.

"It's a beautiful tree, Stephan, and I like it very much!" she exclaimed. Then, without refrain, she hugged him. "Now come on in. I have a hot meal waiting for you," she added.

"Got to take care of these horses first. Come on, son."

Jan returned inside, very relieved that they were home and safe. After setting the table, she waited for the sound of their familiar footsteps on the porch then, while they were freshening up, she took the food she had prepared out of the oven.

They were cold and hungry, and the delicious food radiated its heat throughout their bodies. Stephan complimented her on her cooking abilities and asked politely if he could have more.

"Certainly," she replied, handing him the Swiss steak. "I like to see you eat. It's a sign of good health." She smiled.

He took the bowl of steak and gravy, filling his plate once more, then passed it to his father.

"Can we put the tree up tonight, Jan?" he asked.

"If that's what you want to do, and if it's all right with your father," she answered. She was shocked that he would ask her first instead of his dad.

"Why not?" Bob agreed. "But I'll have to cut some of it off first. I think it's too big for the house." He chuckled.

"Well, I'll leave it to you two to fix a place for it while I clean up the dishes. Can I help you decorate it, Stephan?"

"Sure," he said, beginning to feel the spirit of Christmas.

Bob and Stephan brought the tree decorations down from the attic, then cut the tree to size, and brought it into the house. By the time they had the tree mounted in the stand, Jan had finished the dishes and put some Christmas carols on their small stereo to add to the festive mood.

Later, Bob enjoyed watching the two of them work together, periodically lending a helping hand, but mostly observing. It sent his mind to a different time, and his eyes became moist, remembering his wife and Stephan when they often worked together decorating the Christmas tree.

Christmas had been a happy time for them when Laura was alive. After her death, it became nothing more than a traditional thing. The fiber of the family had been broken. The past three Christmas seasons had been a lonely time for them both. He now watched Jan and Stephan and listened to their cheerful banter, realizing that her presence was bringing back the spark of Christmas joy into their lives. She knelt down to spread a sheet around the base of the tree. Bob saw the colorful lights cast a glowing reflection in her hair. Her beauty and enthusiasm seemed to be shining and caused a deep stirring within him.

For the first time, Jan felt that Stephan's resistance to her was weakening, and she welcomed the change in him. She first felt it when she saw him wave a salute of goodbye earlier that morning, and now he was laughing and joking with her. Was he beginning to accept her? she wondered.

When the tree was finally decorated, they turned to adorning the window and fireplace mantel with left over strings of lights and garlands. When they were finished, Stephan turned them on and extinguished the house lights. The multicolored Christmas lights and the light from the fire enhanced the coziness of the living room and dining room.

Jan stood back to admire it, then placed her hands on her hips and said, "There's something missing." Stephan looked at her with a puzzled expression. "What?" he asked.

"Well, it looks kind of bare under the tree, don't you think?"

"Yeah, but it ain't Christmas yet," Stephan reminded.

"Haven't you ever put presents under the tree before Christmas? We always did..." she said, then stood frozen, with closed eyes, she raised her hands to her head.

Bob moved to her side. "What is it, Jan? Are you okay?"

"Yes...yes...I'm all right, but... For a moment I thought I remembered something."

"Something about Christmas? Try to remember," he urged her.

"I'm trying to," she said, slumping into a chair. "A picture flashed through my mind, but I couldn't hold on to it."

"What was the picture, Jan? Try to remember."

"A child...in a room. There was a Christmas tree with presents all around it. There were two people...a man and woman. They were watching the child open a present, but I couldn't see their faces," she said, closing her eyes. She was trying to recapture the image, to bring it back, but she couldn't.

"Maybe this is a beginning. You may be starting to get your memory back," Bob noted.

"Do you think so? Oh, if only I could remember."

"Yes, I do," he said, trying to be encouraging, even though he felt apprehension at the thought of her remembering. Perhaps it was **her** child she saw, and it was Jan and her husband who were the parents.

Stephan stood beside her. He'd seen her expression change, and he felt a sudden surge of fright. She looked at him and saw the concern on his face. "I'm okay," she reassured him.

"Well," Bob said, rapidly changing the subject, "you two have done a great job of decorating."

Jan looked around her. "Yes...yes, it does look nice." She was trying to compose herself. The fleeting remembrance had frightened her, for it had come on so hastily. "Stephan, I think you deserve a treat for all your hard work. Would you like me to make you some hot chocolate?"

"No, thank you. I'm kinda tired, so I think I'll go to bed."

"Okay, son," Bob said. "I'll be right behind you."

Jan also felt suddenly tired. "That goes for me, too. Good night everybody," she said, then waved as she headed for her room.

Bob waved back, and thanked her for helping with the Christmas decorations, then he sunk into his chair. Could it be that she was starting to get her memory back? He wondered. Many questions would be answered if she were. Answers he may not want to know. He finally got up from his chair, turned off the lights, and reluctantly headed for his bedroom, knowing these questions would plague him all night.

NINE

On Wednesday evening, just before the holiday, Bob was sitting at the table leafing through a magazine, and Jan was busying herself with baking cookies. She placed a flat pan of cookie dough in the oven, set the timer, then moved to the table and sat down across from him.

"I'm working on the last batch of cookies. Would you ask Stephan if he'd like some?"

Bob put his book aside and walked to Stephan's room. He knocked lightly on the door, then opened it. He found him asleep on the bed. He crossed the room quietly, shut the television set off, then placed a blanket over him.

"He's out like a light," he said, returning to the table.

Jan looked at her watch. "I didn't realize it was so late. You know, Bob, he's a good boy. He hasn't missed a day of school, and his grades have been excellent. You've taught him some real values, and I can see the respect he holds for you."

"Yeah, he's got some smarts, all right. I think he got it from his mother, but you've helped him quite a bit yourself."

"Oh, I don't know about that. I think you should give yourself some credit, too. Bob, you're a very intelligent, interesting man," she replied, then, unconsciously, she placed her hand on his.

"I kinda let him down in a way, though," he came back. "Got too liberal in the way we were living, until you came along and straightened us out." He smiled.

She felt her face flush at his praise of her. "You know, I think you're going to win that race you're always talking about."

"There's always hope," he said, feeling the softness of her hand against his. "Old Blue has the blood to run, and I've waited a long time to find just the right horse."

At that moment the oven timer went off, and Jan headed for the kitchen. The touch of her hand on his had aroused him. He listened to her humming and watched her seductive body move about the kitchen. His hunger for her was building, and, though he tried to mask these feelings, it was becoming more difficult.

He rose from the table and walked into the living room, then placed a fresh log on the fire. It was an act to quell the passion within him created by the nearness of her. He couldn't shake what he was feeling, and the atmosphere of the room seemed to be filled with a sensuous ambience.

He sat on the floor in front of the fireplace, his arms wrapped around his legs and watched the flames lick at the fresh log. Was he right? Did she have feelings for him? Only a moment before, they were talking, and she seemed interested in what he had to say, but that was all he could detect in her. He saw nothing in her mood to indicate otherwise.

He looked up, feeling her presence near him. She was standing beside him, looking down with that wide smile and parting her lips. She held a bottle of wine and two glasses in her hands.

"I thought it might be nice to have some Christmas cheer," she said.

He agreed. Taking the bottle from her, he took her hand and assisted her in sitting down. He uncorked the bottle and poured the glasses half full. They sipped the wine sparingly, savoring its flavor.

"This is nice," she said after a moment of silence.

"What's that?"

"Oh, just sitting here. Warm and comfortable, watching the soft Christmas lights, the flickering shadows cast by the fire, and listening to the howling wind outside."

"You sound like a romantic," he said, smiling, but it was only an attempt to defuse his own feelings.

"What's wrong with being a romantic?" Her eyes were fastened to his rugged face.

"Oh...nothing...nothing at all. I was just making a joke."

"Do you think romance is...funny?" she asked softly.

Bob turned his face toward her. Her eyes never wavered from his. They seemed to burn with the same passion he was feeling, and he felt his defenses weakening. He picked up the bottle of wine and refilled their glasses, merely a diversionary tactic, yet his pulse beat rapidly and the heat started creeping up his neck. He could not let his feelings for her override the judgment he had set for himself, but his heart rebelled. He wanted to take her in his arms and tell her all the things that were pent up inside him, but how could he, not knowing what the future held.

Jan's passionate juices were flowing. She looked deep into his soft blue eyes and saw the smoldering longing for her reflected in them. In her mind the stage was set, the mood was right, and they were alone. She would not be denied what she longed to know.

"No...I don't think romance is...funny," he finally said, placing his glass to his lips and taking a sip of wine.

Her mind suddenly went to Kate Donovan. "You know Kate's a very attractive woman, and she's interested--"

"Forget about Kate," he said, interrupting her. Even he was puzzled by his abruptness at the mention of her name. "We're just friends and have been for a long time," he added in softer tones. "I've told you that before, Jan."

"Well, I thought, perhaps it was something more," she said coyly.

"Where did you get that idea? We're close, but never been real close...know what I mean?"

A redness came to his face, and for the first time she realized a shyness in him. She smiled, knowing what he meant, and a feeling of relief filled her heart. "Yes, I just thought--"

"Well, you thought wrong, Jan."

"Maybe you're afraid to make a commitment. Kate certainly wouldn't object."

"Why in the hell are we talking about Kate?" he asked, trying to keep from showing his irritation.

"We're not talking about Kate. We're talking about you making a commitment," she qualified.

"I'm not afraid of making a commitment. Hell, woman, I don't even know what you're talking about," he snapped, the frustration now showing in his voice.

"Then why do you back away from me?" she blurted out, throwing caution to the wind. She was bound and determined to know how he felt about her.

She caught him off guard with her sudden statement.

"What...what do you mean, back away from you?" he asked, then raised himself from the floor and stood with his back to the fireplace.

She got to her feet and stood in front of him with her hands behind her back. "I'm thinking of that awful night with Bill Holt. I know you wanted to kiss me then, but you didn't. And there have been other times, too," she continued, moving closer to him.

"What makes you think I wanted to kiss you? If you remember correctly, you had too much to drink that night. I think you were just imagining things."

She moved closer to him. "I **did** have too much to drink, but a woman knows when a man wants to kiss her. You want to now, but you're holding back. Why?" She pressed her body to him, still looking into his eyes.

Her sweet smell intoxicated him. His eyes traveled over her beautiful face. He sensed the same desire in her. The cautioning voice within him was only a whisper now. He'd passed the limits of his own reasoning. His eyes glazed with passion, he gathered her tightly in his arms and ravished her neck with passionate kisses.

She threw her head back, savoring the ecstacy of the moment. She sensed the pent-up passion within him and surrendered to it, pressing her body tightly against him. Jan felt his heart beating wildly against her breast. She sighed involuntarily with an unmistakable whimper of pleasure when his mouth covered hers once again. Her body was on fire, waiting so long for this moment to be in his arms and to feel his hot, savoring lips upon hers.

Their breathing became erratic when they explored each other. He continued smothering her neck with kisses. She started to unbutton the top button of his shirt, then slowly unfastened them to the waist. She gently ran her fingers through the dark hairs of his chest. She knew in her heart that she'd never experienced this kind of euphoric feeling before. Amnesia or not, this wonderful sensation could never have been forgotten.

They stopped for a moment, staring into each other's fiery eyes. Urgently, she pulled him down to her and kissed his flaming lips long and hard. She felt her body gently lowered to the floor, then felt the caress of his hand on her breast. Lost in the moment of sensuality, she was ready to give herself to this man willingly, no matter what consequences lay ahead.

She listened to his soft, whispering, tender voice. "I love you, Jan. I never thought I would ever love again. You not only moved into my home, you moved into my heart."

"Oh, Bob, I love you too. I don't know how it happened and I don't care. I only know that it did and I'm glad," she said softly.

"I tried not to let it happen. I didn't want to fall in love with you, but I couldn't help myself. You're such a wonderful, inviting woman," he said huskily. They found each other's lips once again, tasting the sweetness of uncontrolled love.

"I know...I know, darling," she cried, clinging to him. She could feel his taut muscles while she ran her hands up and down his back, then into his thick, wavy black hair.

He could feel the urgency of his manhood. "Jan, you're making me crazy. You're so beautiful and I want you so much." But suddenly he jumped to his feet.

"Jan, we can't do this!" he exclaimed.

His sudden movement startled her. "What's wrong?" she asked, disappointment in her voice. She couldn't believe this was happening. Only a moment before he seemed so passionate, and now he was backing away from her again. What was the matter with him? She rose to her feet and stood next to him. "Is it me? Did I do something wrong, or is it Stephan you're worried about?"

He looked into her wide, green eyes. "Oh, Jan, believe me, it's not you. Dammit, it's me."

"What is it?" she asked with a puzzled expression. His face was lined with tension, and his eyes held a look of despair.

"Some day, you'll find out who you really are. And, when you do, you'll have to return to that person's life, whatever it might hold."

She remained silent, not knowing what to say. She stared intently into his eyes, seeing the anguish and torment in them.

"There could be many people who love and care for you, Jan. You may have a husband and children that are worried to death about you. You can't walk away from that possibility. Regardless of how we feel about each other now, when your memory returns, things will change between us. If we let ourselves continue like this, we'll both be hurt."

"Surely if there were people looking for me, we would have some information by now."

"I'm sure Dan's doing all that he can, and I'm convinced there's someone out there looking for you. I tried not to let this happen, but you...you were too much tonight. I've felt this way about you for so long, I guess my defenses were down."

"I had hoped you cared for me, but I wasn't sure how you felt."

"I do love you, Jan, but try to understand my point. It's because of my love for you that I believe there has to be someone in your life who feels the same way about you, and I can't invade that territory. I pride myself being an honorable man, and letting ourselves go completely without a thought of no one else goes against everything I believe in. I was trying to protect you, and myself. You've seemed happy here with us, and I just didn't want to destroy that. Now all I've succeeded in doing is causing you more anguish. I'm sorry, Jan. I hope you'll forgive me. I truly want to have a full relationship with you, but I can't. All I can do is love you within the limits I've set."

She cupped his face with her hands, seeing the agony in his pale blue eyes. "Of course, I forgive you, because I know you're doing this out of love and respect for me. I just wish I could make you believe that there isn't anyone. Don't ask me how I know, I just do," she said firmly, wiping her tears away.

He looked into her determined face, and saw the strength that he so much loved about her.

They sat cuddled before the fire, each lost in their own thoughts. Jan stared into the dancing light of the flames. Questions filled her mind on who she really was, and felt they could surmount anything feeling the way they did.

She felt secure, but Bob had misgivings. He wanted to know everything, and she couldn't blame him. Until he knew she had no attachments, he would never fully express his love for her. The joy of working side by side with him, and knowing that he loved her, would have to be enough.

Bob felt relieved. He had at last expressed his love for her and the thoughts he'd kept to himself. He couldn't believe that she felt the same love for him, a simple rancher, but she did. He found it difficult to comprehend her belief that there was no one in her life. A woman attractive and tender like Jan had to have someone. He wished he could dispel that thought from his mind, but it wouldn't go away.

She turned in his arms to face him. "Can I ask you something?"

"Anything," he replied.

"I would love to help you train Blue."

"I told you before, he's not like Buck. I don't want you getting hurt."

"But, you're going to let Stephan help you. He's just a boy. Aren't you afraid he'll get hurt?" she persisted.

"Stephan has been around stock all his life, its nothing new to him," Bob pointed out.

"I've been riding just about every day. You even said I was a good rider," she said, staring into his eyes.

"I got no argument there, course I had a little something to do with that," Bob bragged, then chuckled.

"Well then..."

"Okay...okay, but first we'll see how you get along with him," he said, then threw two more logs on the fire. They lay for hours nestled in each others arms, listening to the crackle of burning wood in the fireplace and the howling winter wind pelting the house with fresh snow. There was a happiness between them now, a happiness that neither one knew how long would last.

Stephan awoke to find he was still fully dressed and had a blanket thrown over him. The bed felt comfortable to him and he debated whether to lie there or get undressed. He rolled over on his side, gathering the pillow under his head. He heard soft voices in the living room and knew that his father and Jan were still up, but... there was something strange in the sound of their voices. He couldn't make out what they were talking about, and it spurred his curiosity.

He quietly rolled off the bed and opened his bedroom door. Standing in its opening, he still could not make out their words. He moved into the shadow of the hallway. Remaining there, he observed them.

He saw them standing by the fireplace. Jan was standing close to his father and looking up at him. Their words had become softer and he strained his ears to hear. He remained in the hallway in silent shock when he saw his father take her in his arms, then kiss her hard on the mouth. His stomach churned when he watched them. He saw her head go back and his father ravish her neck with kisses while she clung to him. She liked what his father was doing to her. He saw them kissing once more, deep kisses, passionate kisses.

Suddenly his mind was filled with all the things he had seen. The subtle glances his father had bestowed upon her that he thought had gone unnoticed. Helping her around the house, and shaving off the beard he had worn for so long. He continued to listen and watch them, he felt he were being shoved aside when he heard his father tell her she could ride Blue when his training began. A fierce anger settled over him. He felt nervousness within himself. His heart beat so hard he could hear it in his ears, and he realized his worst fears were to become a reality.

Silently he moved back into the sanctity of his room. He was angered and confused. The world he held so jealously around him was crumbling. His father was in love with this woman who came to them from out of nowhere. She had taken over the house, and now she was taking over his father, and soon, his mother's place.

His feelings had been changing in her favor. He was beginning to respect and like her for the things she had done. Now she was only like a viper to him, waiting for the right moment to strike, to come between him and his father, and destroy the memory of his mother. At this moment he hated her, but what could he do? If he questioned their actions, it would gain him nothing. Later when he lay on his bed, tears of disappointment and despair trickled across his cheek. He felt he had nothing, save for the memory of his mother.

He awoke the next morning to the sound of the howling wind. Throwing back the blanket, he went to the window. It was snowing hard, and the wind whipped the snow into a frenzy about the corners of the outbuildings. The first blizzard of the season. He liked the changing seasons and especially the snow. It was a time to build snowmen, forts, and have snowball fights.

He continued to look out the window. He saw the tractor moving away from the barn, pulling a wagon loaded with hay. At the sight of Jan and his father, he suddenly remembered the previous night. It wasn't something he had dreamt, but a reality. He remained in his room throughout the day, watching television and refusing to eat.

Jan was concerned about him, but when she questioned if he didn't feel well, he turned his back to her and said nothing. Why was he acting so strangely? she wondered. Had he somehow learned what had taken place between his father and herself? He couldn't have. Bob had said he was asleep. Had he gotten up? They would have heard him. The house was too small for them not to. She tried to dismiss the thought, but it continued to tug at her. She decided not to pressure him to talk, or mention her feelings to Bob, telling herself that Stephan was probably in one of his moods.

It was dinner time, so Jan fixed a plate of food for Stephan, then asked Bob, "Will you take this plate of food into Stephan? I don't know why, but he's been in his room all day."

"I think he's just got a case of the lazes. He'll be all right."

"He's not a lazy boy, Bob. I've never seen him act this way."

With the food in hand, Bob knocked on Stephan's door, then opened it. Stephan was lying on the bed watching television.

"What's the matter, son?" Bob asked, with concern in his voice.

He continued to stare at the television. "Nothing," he replied.

"Well, Jan fixed you a nice plate of food."

"I don't want it. I'm not hungry," he retorted.

"Now listen, son, you haven't eaten all day. What's the problem?"

Stephan didn't want his father to know that he'd seen them kissing each other or overheard their plans for Jan to help train Blue. He knew if he kept acting this way, his father eventually would guess what was wrong, and he didn't want a confrontation with him. "I don't know. I just don't feel good, Dad." He hoped to sound convincing.

"Well, I want you to try and eat your dinner," Bob urged. "Then, if you're not feeling any better by tomorrow, we'll go in to see Doc Woodward, okay?"

"Okay," he agreed reluctantly. He didn't want to have to go to the doctor's. He wasn't ill physically, only sick in the heart.

When Bob left the room, Stephan eyed the food on his plate. He had only refused to eat, out of anger and stubbornness. The food smelled good and increased his desire to eat. He picked up the fork and took a bite of the stuffing. The flavor stimulated his taste buds and he started eating more rapidly. Finished, he set the plate on the nightstand beside his bed. He could have eaten more, but didn't want to have to face Jan.

To see her would only serve to reinforce his anger with her. His father's broken promise that **he** would be instrumental in training Blue only added fuel to a fire that was already raging inside him. In his eyes, he suddenly meant little to his father. He was picturing the two of them together at the fireplace. He never saw his father kiss his mother the way he was kissing and caressing Jan.

Then it came to him in a sudden rush. He knew exactly what he would do.

TEN

Bob rolled out of bed around eight in the morning. He shaved, showered and performed all the necessary functions one does to prepare himself for the day. He unconsciously started humming and whistling. He hadn't done that in a long time, and he realized a feeling of contentment.

He'd gone against his better judgement, by professing his love for Jan, but she had made him confess by driving him out of his mind with desire. Yes, he loved her, and he couldn't help himself, but he wondered if he hadn't made a mistake.

He felt burdened with reservations of ever having a complete life with her. Her commitment of love for him came easily, but could it be that simple? Surely she had to think of the possibility of a husband, even children. Based on her present feeling, she chose to ignore that possibility, but he could not. He could not pledge himself totally to her, even though his dreams had been filled with wanting, exploring, and making love to her.

He finished dressing and went into the kitchen, expecting to see her, but she had not gotten up yet. He searched the counter for the thermos of coffee she always prepared before retiring. Not seeing it, he presumed she had neglected the task and started preparing the coffee himself.

Jan finally entered the kitchen and saw him staring out the window watching the snow fall. Sneaking up behind him, she ran her fingers around his waist. He jerked at the tickling sensation and grabbed her hands in his. Raising her fingertips to his mouth, he caressed them slowly and tenderly, sending a tingling feeling down her spine. He held her tightly against him, and she laid her head on his back.

"Good morning," he whispered.

"Good morning, my darling," she replied softly. He could feel her soft, warm lips through his shirt.

Releasing her, he turned and engulfed her in his arms. She pressed her body against him, yielding to the moment, and she looked up at him smiling.

"You know, whenever you smile, your whole face lights up, and your beautiful green eyes sparkle," he said, brushing his thumb over her mouth, stealing her breath away. She pushed against his chest with her hands, but he held her close to him. They both knew they were playing with fire by letting their emotions run away with them.

"Remember, honey, we must be careful until we talk to Stephan," she whispered, using any excuse to cool the burning embers between them.

His voice became sensuous. "God, how I love you, Jan, but I know you're right."

Her desire for him was intoxicating. She exhaled her breath in sexual passion, and they parted simultaneously.

Gaining control of themselves, the aroma of boiling coffee caught Jan's attention. "I made coffee last night. Why are you making more?"

"The thermos wasn't on the counter. I figured you just forgot."

"I know I filled it last night," she said, searching through the cabinets.

"That's strange," Bob said. He left the kitchen and went to Stephan's room. When he opened the door, he was surprised by Stephan's absence. Looking around the room, he noticed his chaps were missing.

"Stephan must have taken it," he said, returning to the kitchen. He's not in his room, so he's probably feeding the horses and took the thermos with him. The kid likes his coffee," he added, chuckling.

"Why don't you go out and check on him? I'll start something for breakfast."

Bob put on his heavy winter coat and hat and left the house. Within fifteen minutes, he returned. Jan turned away from the stove and saw a look of concern on his face.

"What's the matter?"

"I think he's skipped out, Jan. His horse is gone. I looked everywhere, and he's not here."

"But where would he go in **this** weather? Maybe he's just checking the herd," she offered, knowing in her heart that this was just wishful thinking. Surely he had seen them that night, she deduced.

"No, he's gone. If he were checking the herd, I'd have seen some tracks. But the snow hasn't been disturbed. I figure he must have left several hours ago."

Jan felt her stomach tighten. "He saw us," she said.

"What are you talking about?"

"He saw us holding each other and kissing the other night in front of the fireplace. That's why he acted so strangely yesterday. He's mad at me, and probably you, too."

Bob slumped into a chair. "I can't understand him. I thought he was beginning to accept you."

"I thought so, too," she said with sadness in her voice. She looked into his worried eyes. "He's so opposed to anyone getting close to you. Bob, we'll never be able to have a complete relationship."

Her words sent a chill through him. "If we don't, it'll not be because of Stephan," he said forcibly.

"But he's been an obstacle all along...you know that. And now he's pulled this stunt to tear us apart." She quickly turned away, not wanting him to see how upset she was becoming.

"I admit, he's a problem, but you can't blame Stephan for all of it," he said, becoming frustrated.

"Who else is there to blame? If his attitude were different"

"Now wait a minute, Jan," he said, racing to her side before she could finish. "It's not all his fault. I'm partially to blame for the way he feels. I should have made him realize that life goes on, that you can't hold on to the past."

"Don't you see, you're doing the same thing to me. Trying to make me think I have someone, a family. I explained my feelings about that. I know there's no one. Stephan's holding on to something that's real in his life, not a maybe. I love you both, and I want us to live as a family."

Bob turned her toward him and saw the moisture collecting in her eyes. His heart went out to her. Drawing her into his arms, he held her close and kissed her tears away. "I know, I know. When I get my hands on that boy..."

"I want you to be understanding and gentle with him," she cautioned. "Talk to him and let him know you understand how he feels. Then maybe he'll come to know your feelings. But first we have to find him."

"Check and see if there's any food missing. If there is, then he's most likely holing up somewhere in the hills, brooding. If not, then he's gone to a friend's house."

Jan made a quick check of the foodstuffs, but she found nothing missing. Bob called all of Stephan's friends, but no one had seen him. He knew Stephan had left hours before. The snow had covered all signs of him leaving. If he were going to a friend's place, he would have reached his destination by now. Panic was setting in. It had been snowing all night, and snowing hard right now. He had to find him, but which direction did he go? There's no way to tell, he thought to himself.

He couldn't wait another minute. He dressed for the cold weather, and Jan prepared food and more hot coffee, just in case he found Stephan out there somewhere. At nine-thirty he left the house, and saddled up Buck to go on the search. He knew it would be slow going with ten inches of new snow on the ground. Not having any idea which direction Stephan could have gone, he took his best guess. He knew Stephan liked the wooded hills, and pointed Buck in that direction.

After Bob had left, Jan decided that keeping busy would help diminish the worrisome thoughts plaguing her mind. She remembered that he'd asked her to wrap some gifts he had bought for Stephan. But when she saw the hunting rifle that Bob had taken so much time to choose, her shoulders drooped and she started to weep uncontrollably.

She had tried so desperately not to come between them, but, by her continued presence, that's exactly what she had done. `Why didn't I leave when I first knew my feelings for him were more than friendship?' she admonished herself. `All of Stephan's pain and worries would never have come to be.' He and Bob would still share that father and son bond she had seen between them when she had first arrived.

Knowing these thoughts were not helping matters, she gradually calmed herself. Could it be so wrong to love someone like Bob? Why isn't it possible for them to become a family? She mulled these questions over and over in her mind.

Stephan lay unable to move because of the pain it was causing him. He felt cold, wet, and frightened. He struggled with his broken leg until most of the pain left. He relaxed and the night lingered on and on. Suddenly he awakened. He must have fallen asleep, he thought, and knew he could not allow that to happen again or he would freeze to death. He started to go over in his mind how he had come to be in this terrible situation.

He had waited until midnight. Feeling confident that they were asleep, he dressed very warm, putting on his stove pipe chaps over his jeans. He stopped when he spotted the thermos. He quickly grabbed it, then silently stole out into the night.

The blizzard had blown itself out, and there were only a few large snowflakes floating listlessly to the ground. A good six to eight inches of snow cover had fallen. He could hear it crunch beneath his boots while walking toward the barn. He saddled his horse and stuffed the thermos into the saddlebags. Leading the horse out of the barn, he mounted the animal, took a last look at the house, and headed out.

He knew a shortcut that would put him in line with his destination. At approximately three miles, he would have to leave the road and go cross-country.

Keeping the animal to a moderate walk, two hours had brought him to Miller's Creek. He dismounted and pulled the thermos from the saddlebags, letting the horse rest while he drank the hot coffee.

Fifteen minutes had passed when he mounted up again. Then he crossed the creek and on up the slope toward its ridge. The animal started to labor, and he felt the horse's footing slip because of the snow. He dismounted, deciding to lead the animal. The snow had been getting heavier and slick, and he found it difficult to get solid footing. He moved slowly upward, pulling on the reins, urging the horse on. Suddenly, his feet flew out from under him. He tightened his hand on the reins, but his reflexes weren't quick enough. The reins slipped through his fingers. He felt himself sliding downward, and put his arms out to slow his descent. But, he continued to slide, and the brush stung his face. He whipped past the branches on the ground which were grabbing at his legs. Finally, it ended. Stephan lay still, for a moment. He could feel his heart beating rapidly. His face stung and his body started to ache. He tried to move, but a searing pain shot up his leg. He relaxed, waiting for the pain to ease. He instinctively put his hand on his leg, and again felt the excruciating pain. He yelled in agonizing pain, but nobody came. He could only feel the falling snow hitting his face.

He knew his leg was broken. The heavy snow continued its relentless downpour. His clothes were getting soaked, and he couldn't move. He lay in the darkened night, and now, because of his broken leg, his plan could not be put into play.

Stephan was becoming exhausted, but he had to keep himself awake. He started to sing songs, and talk to himself, but his efforts failed him. Soon there was only a deafening silence.

The trek became tough on Buck, and Bob stopped many times to give him rest. He tried to survey the area, using binoculars, but with it snowing so hard the lenses would cover quickly.

He continued on upward, reaching the edge of the timbered land. There he looked around, seeing no sign of anyone, not even a hunter. Reaching Miller's Creek, he dismounted and poured himself a cup of coffee. He felt the liquid warm his insides. After finishing the cup of brew, he mounted Buck once again and continued his search; shouting out Stephan's name now and again, hoping for some response.

Stephan suddenly awoke, feeling a burning sensation in his throat, then a gentle warming followed in his chest and abdomen. When he had to cough, it sounded deep, harsh and raspy.

When he tried to get up, he heard a voice. "Take it easy, son. You're going to be all right." The voice sounded strange and Stephan couldn't place it. Struggling, he opened his eyes, but his vision blurred, and he couldn't make out the face. Another voice spoke: "Get some more of that brandy down him."

He tried to spit the burning liquid out, but he felt the hot substance being put to his mouth again, and was forced to swallow. It burned all through his body.

He looked up, his vision almost clearing. Two men were staring down at him. He tried to move, but felt the searing pain in his broken leg. His wide-eyed expression was one of fear and confusion.

"Don't worry, son. Only tryin' to help ya," the man assured him.

The voice was friendly and it calmed him. Stephan gazed about, trying to determine how he had gotten here. He discovered that he was in a large tent. In it's center, sat a large pot-bellied stove. A Coleman lantern, hung by a rope, spewed light throughout the tent. He saw his clothes hanging from a line stretched across the tent. "You were soaked to the skin, boy. When we found you, we didn't know whether you were alive or dead. We got you out of those wet duds, and that's when we discovered your leg was broke. Guess your horse must of throwed ya. We set it as best we could and made a make-shift splint."

"Where's my horse?" Stephan asked eagerly.

"Your horse's fine. We got him tied up outside. Where do you live?" the second man asked.

"My dad owns a horse ranch near here."

"What's your name and your father's name?"

"My dad's name is Bob Malloy and mine is Stephan."

Bob worked his way over ridges and through draws. The afternoon was dragging on, and he knew he should head back to the ranch. He felt the endless searching was useless but better than just sitting and waiting. `The snows not deep in the wooded areas', he thought, so he angled Buck up a small slope which broke into a flat, open area. There he saw a large tent and Stephan's horse tied beside two others. He felt his heart leap into his throat when he recognized the horse. He urged Buck forward, lunging through the snow toward the tent.

He dismounted, shouting out Stephan's name, then he threw the flap of the tent to one side and stepped in. He spotted the two men, then his eyes caught sight of Stephan's prone body. He rushed to his side, saying nothing to the two men. Angered by Stephan's actions, but so glad to see him, the anger passed instantly.

"What was in your head to make you do this, Stephan?"

"You must be Mister Malloy, the boy's father," the older of the two men said. Bob figured him to be in his sixties, the other in his mid-thirties.

"Yes, I am. What the hell's he doing here?" He nodded his head toward Stephan, his tone demanding.

"Now just hold on! No need to get riled up! We found your son this mornin'. His leg's broke..."

"Broken!"

"Yeah, and he was near froze to death."

"I'm sorry," Bob said remorsefully. "I didn't mean to sound...I've just been worried sick about him."

"I can understand that. I've got a kid, too," the younger man said.

"I'm sorry, Dad," Stephan said scarcely above a whisper.

"You sound horrible, son," Bob said. He placed his hand on Stephan's forehead; it felt hot.

The older man extended his hand out to Bob. "I'm Richard Harrison, and this is my son, Gabriel. We call him Gibb for short. It appears we have an emergency on our hands, Mister Malloy, that boy needs medical attention. We've done everything we can, but I think you'd better get him to a doctor. How far's your ranch from here?"

"It's about a four-hour ride by horse."

"Your son couldn't make that kinda trip. We can load up your boy and the horses in our rig and take care of everything in one shot. That way you won't have to come back here to pick up your critters."

"I'm in your debt, sir," Bob said gratefully.

"Nonsense," Richard replied, waving off Bob's comment. "It's a situation that can't be helped. Things can happen."

While Bob helped Stephan dress, Gibb warmed up the four-wheel-drive jeep station wagon and hitched up the trailer. With the horses loaded and Stephan comfortable in the back of the rig, the four of them headed towards Winthrop.

Inside of forty-five minutes, they were entering Doctor Woodward's waiting room. After leaving Stephan in the doctor's capable hands, he went back to the waiting room.

Jan paced the floor, constantly going from window to window, hoping to see them return. The silence of the house became deafening. All she could hear was the constant ticking of the clock on the mantelpiece. "Where are they?" she cried out loud. Bob had been gone for nearly six hours. "Oh, dear Lord, please don't let anything happen to them. I love them both so much. Why...oh, why did I push myself onto Bob? I know Stephan saw us and that's why he ran away."

She couldn't stand the endless waiting any longer, so she decided to make her way to town in the pickup and inform the Marshall of Stephan's disappearance. She quickly put on her coat and western hat.

When Jan opened the front door, she had to duck her head against the fierce wind. While struggling to close the door, she heard the piercing ring of the phone. She rushed back into the kitchen, silently praying for good news.

They put Stephan in the examination room, and Doctor Woodward took x-rays of his leg. When he read the x-ray, he found a splinter in the fibula.

"Your leg was cracked, but not all the way through. I'll put a cast on it. You got crutches?"

"No."

"I'll get you some. You were up to Miller's Creek, in this weather." He grabbed the table and moved it across the room. I'll pull you over here where I can work," Stephan didn't say anything, while Doctor Woodward prepared the cast.

"What were you doing up there in this weather?" Doctor Woodward asked again.

He gazed at the doctor for a few seconds and then covered his eyes with his arm. "Can you give me something for my cold?"

"Soon as I get your leg taken care of." He continued working on the cast.

After a few moments Stephan said, "He's in love with her."

"Who...Kate?"

"No, Jan...I saw them kissing and everything. He even said she could train Old Blue. They don't need me any more," he said, tearfully.

"Of course they need you. You're Bob's son. Is that why you left, because Bob said that Jan could train Old Blue?"

"Yes. My dad and me, we're supposed to train Blue, not Jan."

"Jan can't ride Blue. Bob won't let her, and besides, she ain't got no experience. Not like you...you have been around stock all your life. I wouldn't be in any hurry, the snows not gone yet. When it is, maybe things will change."

Stephan listened to Doctor Woodward and thought about it. He couldn't go anywhere now but home. He stayed silent and watched him finish up the cast.

While it dried, Doctor Woodward examined him further and administered an antibiotic shot for his chest congestion. He called Bob into the examination room. "Stephan's one lucky boy. It's a good thing those men found him when they did. A few hours more and it would have been all over for him, but he's not entirely out of the woods yet. Give him one of these pills every four hours," Doctor Woodward instructed, handing Bob a packet of sample pills. "His chest is tighter than a gnat's ass stretched over a boulder. Got to get that congestion busted up. Call me tomorrow evenin' and let me know how he's doin'."

"Will do...can I use your phone? I should call Jan."

"Yep, use the phone in the outer office, and take the boy with you. When you get through with your call, come back, I want to talk to you," Doctor Woodward said.

After the call to Jan, Bob went back to the examination room to see Doctor Woodward.

"Is something more wrong with Stephan?"

"Outside of his broken leg and a cold, he's fine." Doctor Woodward was silent for a moment, then he repeated what Stephan had told him.

"There's something else, what is it?" Bob questioned.

"When I put you and Jan together for a few days, I figured to move you off of dead center. I know how Stephan is, and I thought a woman around the house might make a difference in the boy. I had it in mind that you would go after Kate...instead you went for Jan. The boy says you're in love with her, are you?"

"Pardon me! I hate to tell you this, but it's none of your business."

"The boy says it is. I'm sorry, but I'd do somethin' about it before it's too late. She hasn't got her memory back. Suppose she's married and has children?" Doctor Woodward asked.

"Don't you think I've thought about that? What kind of life did she live? I don't know, but somebody has too." Bob argued.

"You love her?"

Bob looked at Doctor Woodward for a moment. "Yes, but I wouldn't deny her husband, or a child if there is any."

"There's something else. I found a shoe with the heel torn off and a bracelet."

"Where?"

"I found them both at Big Craggy Ridge, here I show you." Woodward went to his desk and took out the bracelet.

Bob glanced at the bracelet and turned it over. "The name Melissa, doesn't mean anything. It could be anybody's, and the manufactures of the bracelet are in New York. That doesn't mean anything either, they're shipped all over the world. Melissa...I just don't know."

"That's why I didn't tell you till now. I still have some checkin' to do. I'll run her name through the Internet and see what comes up."

"Okay, but I don't think you'll find anything. I've got to get this boy home and in bed. If you find out anything, let me know."

At eight o'clock they pulled up to the ranch, and Jan quickly opened the door. When Bob and the two men carried Stephan into the house, she could see how pale he looked. She had prepared his room for him, putting extra blankets on his bed. He looked at her through fever-laden eyes, and she tucked the blankets around him. "Foolish boy, running away like that," she said, shaking her head.

He quickly turned his face away from her, but not before she saw the anger he still felt toward her.

When he coughed, she could hear the deep rattle in his chest. It pained her to see him sick like this, but it pained her more, feeling his dislike for her. Still, in spite of things, she remained by his bedside.

When Stephan finally went to sleep, Jan quietly slipped out of his bedroom. She walked into the living room and saw that Bob and the two men were gone. She went to the window and saw the headlights of the vehicle. The snowflakes swirled when they were caught in the beams of the headlights. The vehicle started to move away, and she saw Bob walking toward the house. She moved to the door to let him in.

"How's Stephan?" he asked, shrugging off his coat.

"He's asleep. But his breathing sounds terrible, Bob."

He reached into his coat pocket and removed the sample pills that Doctor Woodward had given him. "Doc says to give him these. He's to get one every four hours."

Bob followed her into the kitchen and wrapped his arms around her. She turned to face him. Looking into his tired eyes, she saw his love for her, but she gently pushed him away.

"What's the matter?" he asked, puzzled by her rejection. "It's been such a horrible day that I just wanted to hold you in my arms and feel your warmth."

"What's wrong is us! Your boy is lying in there with a broken leg and sick," she said with harshness. "No. I'm saying we should have been more careful. We both know what his feelings are, but we didn't care. We were caught up in our own emotions. I'm the one who pushed you into admitting your love for me. I had to know...and I'm responsible for what has happened."

He took her in his arms once again and held her close to him. Speaking softly, he tried to ease her qualms. "No...no, Jan. What he did was on his own. He has to take the responsibility for that. You have treated that boy like he was your son. Your being here has been the best thing that has happened, for him...and me since Laura passed away."

They stood silently for a few moments, holding each other. Bob kissed her cheek and felt the moisture of a tear upon his lips. He loved this woman, and he wanted her intensely. His mind reeled with desire for her. His heart told him to take her in full communication of his love, but his mind urged caution, for he knew not what the future held for them.

Jan felt the warmth of his body penetrate her being. But she could not respond to the need she felt within him.

His words remained in her mind, but she couldn't shake the feeling that she was responsible for what had happened to Stephan. She removed her arms from around him. "I'd better check on Stephan," she said softly.

While she checked Stephan, Bob thought about what Doctor Woodward had told him. Stephan confessed everything to the doctor. Why he had run away and his feelings toward Jan. He also, informed him that he had found a bracelet with the name Melissa stamped on it. He planned to do more checking and would let him know if he found anything more, which Bob doubted. Now she's agreed to stay until we race Old Blue. After that, we'll see what happens, he said to himself.

Bob walked into Stephan's room. "How's he doing, Jan?"

"He seems to be resting peacefully," she replied.

"Doc gave him a shot. Maybe it's starting to work. I think we should get some rest."

When they were outside his room, he placed his hands on her shoulders and drew her close to him. After kissing her gently, he gazed into her green eyes. "Goodnight, Jan, thank you for being such a gentle and caring woman."

She smiled. "Goodnight, Bob, and thank you for being that special person you are."

ELEVEN

On the morning before Christmas, sixteen inches of new snow had dropped overnight, and it was still snowing. The cattle crowded the corral next to the barn, bawling for feed. Bob stoked the fireplace with fresh wood, knowing he had to take care of them.

Both he and Jan had awakened earlier than usual. She stepped into Stephan's room to check on him. He was lying on his side, facing her with his eyes closed.

"Are you awake, Stephan?" she asked softly.

He opened his eyes. They appeared to be glazed, and his cheeks were abnormally red. He looked at her for only a moment, then closed them. He also appeared to be struggling with his breathing. He wheezed loudly when ever he sucked in air. When he coughed, it was hard and his face turned fiery red. Her expression was one of anguish, for she could feel his pain. Again, she placed her hand on his forehead. She rushed out of his room, not knowing what to do, and confronted Bob.

"We have to do something. Stephan's worse and he's burning up with fever. I think he has pneumonia."

"All we can do is call Doc Woodward, and there's three feet of snow out there, which means anything with wheels isn't moving. Besides, I wouldn't take a chance trying to get him into town with these conditions. If I got stuck, he'd be in worse trouble." Jan ran to the phone and nervously dialed the doctor's number.

After hanging up the phone, she turned to Bob.

"What did he say?" he asked anxiously.

"He said to keep giving him the pills and give him some aspirin. If the aspirin doesn't work, give him an alcohol bath or apply cold towels to him. We have to get his temperature down or he could go into convulsions."

Bob was filled with anxiety when he followed Jan into Stephan's room. She woke him gently, then slipped the thermometer under his tongue. Waiting the required time, she pulled it from his mouth. He had a temperature of 104 degrees.

"I'll get him some aspirin, and the Doctor says to feed him plenty of broth," Jan said leaving the room.

She took two aspirin from the container and drew a glass of water. She hurried back to the bedroom. "If you'll give this to him, I'll start making some broth. Don't worry, he'll be fine," she added, trying to be encouraging.

Bob gave the aspirins and water to Stephan, then came back to the kitchen. "Jan, I hate to burden you with Stephan, but I've got to feed those cattle. Can you look after him?"

She looked at him quizzically. His voice sounded apologetic for having to impose on her. She wished he weren't so damned prideful. She was more than willing to watch over him. He didn't need to ask, particularly after they had confessed their feelings for each other, and Stephan was part of that package.

"If you'll wait until I get this broth down Stephan, I'll help you feed the cattle."

"I would rather you stay with him. I've never seen him this sick before. I'm afraid he's not going to have a very good Christmas this year."

"We'll just delay it until he's well enough to enjoy himself," she replied.

Bob put on his insulated boots and heavy coat, buttoning it securely around his neck. He walked to where she was standing and looked eagerly into her tender eyes. "I want you to know that I love you very much, and...I don't know what I'd do without you."

A warm glow filled her when she looked up at him and smiled.

"Your cattle are calling you."

"I know," he said in an exaggerated voice of disgust. "But I'll see you later."

"Is that a threat or a promise?" she asked, trying to lighten the moment a little.

"That, my dear, is a **promise**," he emphasized, leaving the house.

Jan took the chicken broth she had prepared to Stephan. He was lying on his stomach, his eyes closed.

"Stephan, are you awake?" she asked. He opened his eyes, but would not look at her. "Sit up, Stephan. I've brought you some broth and your pill."

He slowly sat up, but avoided her eyes. Handing him the cup of broth, she sat beside his bed. Ignoring the fact he wouldn't look at her, she asked, "Are you feeling any better?" He didn't answer. She reached out to feel his forehead, but he moved away from her outstretched hand. She drew it back and continued to watch him. She was becoming more and more frustrated. Couldn't he see she was only trying to help?

"I know why you're upset, Stephan. You saw your father kissing me the other night, didn't you?"

He continued to sip at the broth, keeping his eyes straight ahead, ignoring the question. "You're mad at me right now, and I don't need to tell you why. You know the answer to that as well as me and your father. I know you want to be happy, but think of your father. Wouldn't you like him to be happy, too? I've never said or done anything to hurt you, Stephan, but I think you're being cruel and selfish."

She stood up to leave the room. "I'll be back in a little while to check your temperature. Be sure to take that pill."

Later she returned and took his temperature once again. It continued to read 104. The aspirin was having no effect. Remembering what Doctor Woodward had said, she searched the medicine cabinet for rubbing alcohol. Finding it, she threw the blankets from him. She saw his glassy stare when he looked at her. His cheeks were flushed, and he had offered no resistance when she unbuttoned his pajama top. Using a soft cloth, she doused it with the alcohol and applied it to his body.

Later, when she looked out the living room window, she could see the wind whipping the snow into deep drifts and it depressed her. They were trapped. There was no way they could get Stephan the medical attention he so needed.

Bob worked late into the afternoon feeding the cattle. He dumped bales of hay from the loft into the feeding trough that stretched 300 feet along the length of the barn. It was a time-consuming chore and he missed Stephan's help. He had thought Stephan was beginning to look upon Jan in a different light. Then, all of a sudden, he changed direction and ran away. Where in the hell did he think he was going? He loved him and was worried about him, but at the same time he was irritated with him.

The cattle crowded the trough, pushing and shoving one another to get to the feed. He continued to drop bales through the feeding holes, making sure the feed would last through the night. He still had to tend to his horses, but would save that chore until later. He was getting anxious to return to the house and learn if there was any improvement in Stephan's condition.

He entered the house and was hanging up his hat and coat, when Jan came out of Stephan's room.

"How is he?" he asked worriedly.

"His fever dropped a little after I gave him an alcohol bath, but his breathing seems to be getting worse. I hope those pills take effect soon," she replied.

"Is he awake?"

"He may be. He just lies with his eyes closed. He doesn't try to talk, or at least he won't talk to me."

"When he gets well, we're going to straighten him out on a few things. What he did was foolish and now he's paying for it."

"Yes, he was foolish. But I'm worried that he's having so much trouble breathing, Bob. I just don't know what to do for him."

"Has he been eating?"

"I've been giving him broth and he's taking it."

"Well, I'll go in and see him." Their eyes met for a moment. The concern for Stephan was present in both their minds.

Stephan was lying on his side when Bob entered the room. His mouth was open, and heavy wheezing could be heard when he drew in his breath. He felt the cool touch of his father's hand upon his forehead. He opened his eyes, but only for a moment.

"How are you feeling, son?"

Stephan's eyes remained closed, but he shrugged his thin shoulders. Then he pointed his finger to his mouth and shook his head from side to side, indicating that he couldn't talk. Bob could see that he was having trouble breathing, and he tucked the blankets around him, then left the room.

Jan had prepared a light dinner and was setting the table for them when he entered the dining room.

"Stephan still feels hot," he said when they sat down. "I can remember my father saying the best way to get rid of a cold is to sweat it out. Maybe we should give him something to make him sweat," he added, reflecting back to when he was a boy.

The worry over Stephan was evident in his eyes. Stephan wasn't getting any better and they both knew it.

While Jan did up the dishes from dinner, Bob set about making some lemonade. He added a shot of whiskey to it and took it in to his son. Stephan's blurred eyes gazed up at his father when he entered the room.

"Heck of a Christmas Eve, isn't it, son?"

Stephan nodded his head slightly. Then Bob helped him to a sitting position. "I have something that'll make you feel better," he said, handing the cup to him.

Stephan made a funny face when taking his first sip of the lemonade and tasting the whiskey in it. Finally finishing it, he slid into a prone position. Bob made sure he was adequately covered and left the room.

The outdoor light, mounted at the peak of the barn gable, cast its light through the falling snow. Jan stood at the living room window watching. Bob approached her and cradled her in his arms. She leaned her back against him, laying her hands upon his.

"When is this snow ever going to stop?" she asked.

"It's the worst I've seen in several years. Normally we don't get this much snow," he replied, brushing his lips across her cheek.

"It's odd. When you look at country snow scenes in magazines and on Christmas cards, they always depict something pleasant, something beautiful. We should be enjoying this snow, but instead, it scares me. I wish it would go away."

"It's because of Stephan, isn't it?"

"Yes. We are trapped here because of this snow. He should be in a hospital where he could receive proper care," she said, releasing herself from his arms.

"Maybe the hot lemonade will help him. When does he get his next pill?"

"At eight o'clock. Then one at midnight and that's it. We don't have any more."

After Bob put another log in the fireplace, he took his coat and hat from the peg by the door.

"Where are you going?" she asked.

"I haven't fed the horses, and I want to put fresh straw in their stalls. It'll help keep them warm."

While the night wore on, Jan would periodically check on Stephan. She had given him the last pill and took his temperature; it had dropped another degree. She was thankful for that. The lemonade mixed with whiskey was having some effect. Stephan was sweating profusely and kept removing the blankets. She stationed herself beside his bed, keeping him covered and applying a cool washcloth to his forehead. When he would cough, it was a harsh, unbearable sound. It tore at her heart to see him gasping for air and the expression of pain on his face. She could do nothing to comfort him.

Stephan would have moments of calm, and during those moments, she found herself drifting off. While she dozed, an image of a sick child came into her mind. A man was rubbing something on the child's chest and it had a distinct smell. Then the man wrapped her chest in towels. He held a teaspoon to her mouth. It was sugar, but had something with it that tasted bad. Then the man made her lie down and covered her with a flowered quilt. He kissed her on the forehead, then faded from the room.

Jan suddenly awakened. She remembered the flowered quilt, and knew she had been dreaming of herself as a child. The man in her dream must have been her father, but she could not put a face with him. She tried desperately to recall that one incident in her life. She wondered why she could remember the quilt, but not her father's face. What was the substance he had rubbed on her chest? She knew from her dream that it was sugar he had her swallow, the taste was that familiar, but what did it have in it? She couldn't remember and it disturbed her greatly.

She shoved the dream from her mind and turned her attention to Stephan. He was asleep. She touched his forehead. He still felt hot, but had ceased sweating.

She could see it was starting to get light when she glanced out the bedroom window. It was Christmas morning, but she felt no joy when she left the bedroom. The day was not going to turn out the way she had pictured in her mind.

Bob had fallen asleep in one of the easy chairs. He was awakened when he heard her preparing breakfast.

"Did you get any sleep at all, Jan?"

"I dozed, off and on," she answered, pouring him a cup of coffee.

"It finally quit snowing," he said, looking out through the dining room window. When she placed the cup in front of him, he took her small hand in his.

She pulled her hand from him and went back to the stove. He noticed the lack of response to him, but he said nothing. He observed her while she worked silently at cooking breakfast. She seemed distant, preoccupied. Had this situation with Stephan given her a change of heart? he wondered.

Setting the breakfast on the table, he waited until she joined him. She avoided his eyes, and he suddenly felt emptiness in his heart. Something had changed in her attitude. She seemed to have no interest in him. He wanted to question her, but was reluctant to do so. If she were changing her mind about the two of them, maybe it was for the best, he thought.

He finished the last of the bacon and eggs on his plate and washed it down with his coffee. "I've got to get busy feeding the stock," he said as he stood up.

"Coal oil and lard! That's what it was!" she shouted, looking at him.

"What the hell are you talking about?" he asked in confused tones.

Jan explained the dream she had had, and that she'd been trying to remember what had been used to break up the congestion in her as a small child.

Once he realized why she had seemed so distant and uninterested in him, a feeling of relief raced through his heart. "Rub a mixture of coal oil and lard on his chest? I've never heard of that before," he said.

"It must have been an old-time remedy that my father knew about. He also put some on sugar and made me swallow it."

"Are you sure?" he asked.

"Yes, I am positive," she replied. "I'd like to try it on Stephan."

"Putting in on his chest may be all right, but giving it to him internally...I don't know," he mumbled hesitantly.

"It didn't kill me. But I won't give it to him unless you approve of it."

"The pills haven't worked. Neither did the whiskey. Let's try it."

Jan drained the bacon grease from the frying pan into a bowl while Bob extracted some coal oil from a lantern. Mixing the two ingredients, they applied it to Stephan's chest, then wrapped him in towels. She applied two drops of the oil to a teaspoon of sugar. Stephan accepted it, but not willingly.

That evening they were resting in the living room. Tears filled Jan's eyes while she watched Bob gazing into the flickering fire. He looked sad and deep in thought. Her heart went out to him, for she knew his concern for Stephan was deepening. She wanted to comfort and give herself to him in that special intimate way, but knew that could not happen until Stephan was well and willing to accepted her.

Whenever there were close moments between her and Bob, she could see the doubts written on his face. Even if there were someone in her past, like he suspected, she'd questioned herself whether she could ever return to him, knowing the ever-building desire and love that consumed her heart for Bob.

Jan knelt down next to him and grasped his warm hand.

"Bob, Stephan is going to get through this. I just know he is."

He looked into her fervent green eyes, wanting desperately to believe. "I hope you're right, Jan. At first I was so angry with him for running away and putting us through this that I just wanted to shake him. Now I'm so terribly scared for him. If I lose him, too, I don't think I could go on living."

Jan saw a tear slowly trickle down his cheek. She cupped his face in her small hands.

"Now you listen to me! We are **not** going to lose that boy. When he's well, we're going to train Blue and win that race. Then all your dreams are going to come true."

"All but one, Jan. And that's having you a part of my life forever."

Jan became angry. She had tried so hard to understand his feelings, but she was becoming tired of his stubborn ideas of another man in her life. She sat for a moment, trying to compose herself, knowing he was so desperately worried about his son.

"Bob, why can't you believe me when I say there is no one in my life? I can't explain it, but I know no man could have ever made me feel as secure and desirable as you do. When you look at me with those tender blue eyes, my heart almost explodes. Why are you being so headstrong about this?"

He smiled and caressed her face with his hand. "In case you don't realize it, you are a very beautiful, elegant, lady. I can't imagine you not having some man going out of his mind searching for you. Someone a lot more appealing then me."

She wanted to argue the point further, but Stephan's harsh cough was heard and their conversation was totally forgotten when they raced to his room.

"It sounds like his congestion is breaking up," Bob said enthusiastically.

Stephan was sitting up. He had taken one of the towels from his chest and was using it to cough into.

"That stuff you gave him did the trick, Jan! His chest is really loosening up. Let's give him another rubdown with it."

She quickly left the room to prepare more of the coal oil and lard. When she came back, they were talking and Stephan's voice sounded much better. Removing the remaining towels, she dipped her fingers into the bowl of solution and rubbed it into his chest. Stephan said nothing to her, but she could feel his cold eyes staring at her.

TWELVE

Stephan was recovering nicely from his bout with pneumonia. With his indifference toward Jan, even while he was so ill, he wondered why she continued to give him care. He knew deep in his heart that, had it not been for her, he possibly could have died. He was thankful she was there for him, but how could he tell her he was sorry and ask her forgiveness? He had taken his anger too far. She had watched over him like his own mother would have, and, after the way he had responded to her, he felt she would never find it within herself to forgive him.

Jan felt she had lost the battle to win Stephan's affection, even as a friend. His apathy to her was beginning to have a heart-rending effect on her. She loved Bob, but without Stephan's acceptance, what kind of a relationship could she hope for? It seemed that her leaving the ranch was the only solution. Maybe then they could start to rebuild their strong bond.

It hadn't snowed in several days, and, due to a warming trend, the roads became derivable. It was the first opportunity to make a trip into town. Stephan's condition had improved, but Jan thought it necessary for him to see Doctor Woodward, and there were food supplies that were needed.

Upon their return, Bob pulled the pickup close to the house so he could carry Stephan in. Stephan gathered the crutches Doctor Woodward had given him under his arms and hobbled to his bedroom.

"I'll bring the groceries in," Bob said, heading out to the pickup. Jan started putting things away. Bob helped her, then went to the barn to tend the horses.

Stephan's thoughts were running wild. Bob had informed the doctor of the unusual treatment Jan had used to make Stephan better. The doctor reaffirmed what Stephan already knew. Had it not been for her, he probably would be in the hospital, fighting for his life. It was time to forget his hostilities and try to make amends with this woman who had tried to be his friend from the beginning.

Jan entered the room, but ignored his eyes when she set a roll and a cup of hot chocolate on the nightstand. She was about to leave, when he reached out and grabbed her wrist.

"Jan...don't go," he stammered.

"Why shouldn't I? You've made it abundantly clear that you don't want me here," she replied coldly, while trying to free herself from his grasp.

He gripped her arm tighter. "Please...stay," he begged. "I know that I have a lot of explainin' to do."

Jan could see the pleading look in his eyes. "Okay, so explain."

Stephan looked long and hard at her, then instantly let the words of remorse flow out in a rush.

"Oh...I'm so sorry, Jan. I'm sorry for everything. But mostly for the way I've treated you. I wanted to apologize, but I didn't know how to start. I couldn't even look at you because I was so ashamed."

"Oh? What changed your mind so suddenly?" she asked, her tone still cool.

"The doctor said you saved my life. If it hadn't been for you, I would've just gotten worse. I don't blame you for being mad at me, I deserve it," he added, dropping his head.

Jan placed her hand under Stephan's chin and lifted his face. All the anger she was feeling seemed to vanish. Looking into his teary eyes, she saw that he was asking her to forgive him. She sat on the bed beside him and took him into her arms. "I'm not mad at you, Stephan, just hurt. I've done everything I could to make you like me. I thought at one point you did, and now I just don't know."

He cleared his throat and nervously started to clutch the blankets.

"I do like you, Jan, but I got mad when I saw you and Dad kissing. You thought I was asleep, but I saw and heard everything. When I heard Dad say you could work Old Blue, I was so hurt I didn't know what to do."

"And that's why you ran away, because of Blue?" she asked.

"It was everything. Dad had promised me I could work him. Are you really in love with my Dad?"

She was taken by surprise with his direct question. "He's a good man," she said hesitantly.

"Are you...going to marry him?" Stephan asked anxiously.

Jan could see a tormented look on his pale face.

"Do you think if we got married I would be taking your mother's place?" she asked knowingly.

"Yes," he answered sheepishly. "I loved my mother. I don't want to forget her, and I don't want Dad to forget her."

"Stephan...Stephan," she said, holding him tightly against her. "No one could ever take your mother's place. She'll always remain your mother, and you'll never forget her. She has a special place in your heart and memory, just as she will always remain a part of your father. No one can ever take that away from either of you, or should want to."

"Is my dad in love with you?" Stephan asked, almost in a whisper.

Jan could tell that the questions he was proposing to her were hard for him. "He says he is," she replied, smiling.

"You never said you were in love with him. Are you?"

She could only stare at him, knowing that, if they were ever to be friends she must be honest.

"Yes...very much so. I'm sure I don't need to tell you what a kind and thoughtful man your father is."

"Well, if Mom has a special place in Dad's heart, that must mean he still loves her."

"I'm sure he does, Stephan. Just as I know how much he loves you."

Stephan was confused by what she was trying to explain to him. "Then how can he be in love with you at the same time?"

Jan thought for a moment before answering. "He has a special love for your mother. He says that he loves me, and I believe him. But it's a different love than he shared with your mother. The love you shared with your mother is different than the love you share with your father, isn't it?"

Until this moment, Stephan had not thought of his love for his parents in this way. His mind finally grasped what she was explaining. He loved his parents, but each of them in his own way.

"I think I understand now. I guess it was pretty dumb of me to do what I did...huh?"

"Well...it certainly was an impulsive thing to do. Where did you think you were going anyway?"

Stephan's face reddened. He didn't expect that question. He could have avoided the truth, but his conscience wouldn't allow him. Hesitantly, he answered:

"I was tryin' to get to Kate Donovan's place."

A surprised look came over Jan's face and her eyes widened. "Why on earth would you go to her?"

"I know she likes Dad a whole lot. I thought she might cause trouble between you and Dad if she knew you'd been kissin' and stuff."

"So you were going to use her to drive a wedge between your father and me, hoping that I would get jealous and leave. Was that your idea?"

"Yeah, and I know now that it wouldn't have worked. All I ended up doin' was gettin' hurt and causin' you and dad a lot of worry."

Jan smiled at the innocence of his plan. She could only imagine what must of been going through his mind when he saw her and Bob, and the hurt he must have felt at thinking he wouldn't have a hand in training Blue. She planted a soft kiss on his cheek, then straightened the blankets. "Well, your leg will heal, and now other matters can start to heal, too," she said, thinking of the relationship between he and Bob.

"Jan, there's still something I have to tell you," Stephan said nervously.

"There's more?" she asked, wondering what else he could possibly have to tell her.

"Remember Bill Holt?"

"Yes...I remember," she replied, thinking of that horrible night.

Stephan looked directly into her questioning eyes. "I put him up to askin' you to go to that dance with him."

"You? How?"

Stephan proceeded to explain the measures he had used to goad Bill into asking her for a date.

She was hurt at the lengths he had gone to trying to rid her from their lives. But, knowing that he was being straightforward with her, helped to wash away some of that hurt. "You were certainly a busy little man, weren't you?"

"Well, when you came to live with us, you changed everything. And then my dad started doin' things, like helpin' you around the house just the way he did when Mom was still with us. Sometimes I would see how he was lookin' at you when you weren't payin' attention. I didn't like it, and I got scared."

"Are you still scared now that you know how your father and me feel about each other?" she asked, cautiously.

"I don't think so. You kind of explained things so I could understand, but sometimes I just don't understand grownups."

Stephan felt her arms tighten around him once more and he responded to her warmth. She touched her lips to his forehead. He looked up and saw her misty eyes.

"Honey, sometimes grownups don't understand themselves," she said, smiling at him.

When she left his room, Jan felt a heavy weight suddenly had been lifted from her shoulders. Until now, she hadn't realized the emotional stress that she had been under. She was relieved, knowing that Stephan didn't object to his father's love for her, or hers for him. She pictured herself a part of them, belonging to something her senses told her could never have existed in her past.

She entered her room and saw all the wrapped Christmas packages that had never been placed under the tree. Now it was time. Stephan was well again, and his confession of affection for her only enhanced her feeling of well-being. She was now truly happy.

After placing the presents under the tree, she entered Stephan's room once more.

"I think it's time to have our Christmas, don't you?"

"Can we...tonight?" he responded excitedly, reaching for his crutches. "Will you put my presents under the tree for me? And Dad has some in his room," he added.

"I'll help you with yours, but I think I'll let your father bring out his own."

After picking up Stephan's presents, she turned and saw a sadness in his eyes.

"What's the matter, honey?"

"Jan, there's nothing for you from me."

She smiled. "Stephan, your friendship is the greatest Christmas gift I could ever receive."

He flushed with embarrassment at her statement. "I can't believe you feel that way after the way I treated you."

Wanting to break the tenseness of the moment for him, she said, "What do you say we forget about all that and get these presents under the tree?"

When they both entered the living room, Stephan's eyes widened in surprise at seeing the amount of gifts already under the tree.

"Now all we have to do is wait for your father to come in from the barn."

"Boy, is he going to be surprised when he sees this," Stephan said happily.

"Pleasantly, I hope," she responded, anxiously awaiting to tell Bob of the new-found relationship between them.

The warm chinook winds and rain melted the winter snows away, and a routine settled over the ranch. Stephan was back in school-- his leg had mended nicely-- Jan and Bob tended to the cattle and horses, and Old Blue was to start training.

Bob had marked off a flat area to be used as a training track, but the ground had not dried enough to allow its use. In the meantime, he used the large open area of the barn to give Blue the exercise he needed. It was important to build his stamina.

Occasionally, Jan rode Buck when Bob worked Blue. They had made several rounds inside the large barn, then Bob pulled Blue to a stop. "Well, you think you're ready?"

"Ready for what," she answered.

"Ready to give old Blue a turn around the barn," he smiled.

It was a surprise to her and it showed in her eyes. She wanted to ride Blue but promised herself she would not ask, she'd done that before. Jan resigned herself to waiting and let him make the offer. Now that he had, she felt some apprehension. **Really!** She exclaimed. "Yes...I never thought you would let me."

"I think you can handle him. Just be careful," he cautioned, when he dismounted.

Jan dismonted and held Blue's reins while he transferred the saddle from Buck. When Bob finished saddling Blue, she expertly mounted him.

"Better grab a handful of mane, Jan."

"Why?"

"You'll see," he said, letting go of the bridle.

She wondered if she hadn't made a mistake in asking to ride him. She could feel the power of this animal just sitting in the saddle, and she knew instantly the difference between Blue and Buck.

Her first impulse was to get off of him, but her pride wouldn't let her. She couldn't let Bob see the apprehension in her face and attempted to mask it. Wrapping a portion of Blue's mane in her hand and grasping it firmly along with the reins, she applied her heels to Blue's flanks.

His sudden start slammed her buttocks into the high-backed cantle of the saddle, yanking the mane out of her hand. She was off balance, leaning out of the saddle when Blue made a sharp turn at the end of the barn.

Seeing she was in trouble, Bob darted toward Blue to intercept them. Jan regained her balance, while they raced along the long portion of the open area. The opposite end of the barn was coming up fast, and again Blue made a sharp turn, throwing dirt against the walls when his hooves dug into the ground.

Jan pulled up on the reins, and brought Blue to a prancing walk. The horse's neck was arched, and he held his tail high. His nostrils flared a bright red, he flipped his head from side-to-side. She felt the tenseness of the animal transmit right through the saddle and into her body. She knew if she relaxed the reins, he would take off on a dead run again.

Bob grabbed the bridle and put his arm out to assist her. "Are you all right?" he asked hesitantly.

"Yes. But he really surprised me. I didn't expect him to move so fast."

Bob still had his arm around her, and he could feel her trembling body against him. He pulled her to him and embraced her, then felt his own body tremble when he held her. "God, you scared the hell out of me, Jan," he said, gently running the back of his hand down her silky cheek.

She felt the heat of his hand against her cheek when he spoke to her in soft, concerned words. With the strength of his arms embracing her, the fear she felt vanished. It was hard to be afraid when Bob was near. She felt a closeness to him and it aroused her. Their eyes met, searching for some unspoken message. His eyes dropped to her mouth, and she felt the impact of the look, like it was a long, lingering kiss. Again, she felt the same pounding in her chest, and she wondered if he had the same awakenings.

"Are you sure you're okay?" he asked, with tenderness in his voice.

"Yes, I'm fine," she replied.

He slowly and reluctantly released her. "I don't think we should try that again."

"Why not? I'll know what to expect the next time."

"You sure you want to ride him again?"

"That was definitely a thrill. Yes, I want to ride him again. I like the feel of his power under me."

"I think you have a little bit of daredevil in you, Jan," he said, admiring her spirit.

March came in with its traditional winds, and Bob had been checking the ground every day, anxious to work Blue on his speed. The days still held a chill, but the winds dried the ground sufficiently that the track could be used.

All winter long Blue had been fed a mix of alfalfa and rye grass, with very little grain. When training started on the makeshift track, his diet would be changed to timothy and larger portions of mash and grain.

Bob worked him longer and harder in the coming days, and Blue received bigger portions of feed. Jan sensed a difference in Blue. He was becoming more difficult to control. He wanted to do the thing he was bred for...running.

After the morning feeding was done, Jan and Bob took their usual coffee break before working Old Blue. Jan said, "Blue is a lot different since you've been working him. He acts like he's more difficult to control."

"That's because he's high on grain. Most horses get that way when you grain them. I want to see what kind of time we can get out of him this morning.

He saddled Blue with the racing saddle, which he hadn't used before.

"You mean you're going to sit on that little piece of leather," she said, eyeing the saddle.

"That's it," Bob said.

"You're just full of surprises. How are you going to stay in that thing?" She wondered.

"Probably with great difficulty," Bob joked, as he tied a small woven rope around Blue's neck.

"What's that for?"

When the gate opens, two things can happen. I'll go flying off over his back end, or, if I'm lucky and hold onto the reins, he'll stop. The rope is to keep me from doing both."

Jan looked at him with a smirk, and said, "You're kidding me."

"I'm not joking, Jan. When that gate opens, he'll be off like a shot."

Bob took Blue's reins and led him out of the barn to the single starting gate. Backing Blue into it, he told Jan to close the gate. The gate secured, Jan mounted Buck and took her place 440 yards up the track.

Jan, with a stop watch in one hand and a rope tied to the starting gate latch in the other, she eyed the gate.

Bob gripped the reins and rope tightly, poised and ready. Suddenly the gate flew open. Blue shied back at the sound of the opening gate and reared up on his hind legs. Bob brought his heels in hard against Blue's flanks and suddenly lost contact with him. He dropped from under him, and rapidly darted out of the gate, reaching for ground, digging at it with his powerful front legs. In two lunges he was at top speed.

Bob thought he had been prepared, but Blue's explosive acceleration took him by surprise. He was suddenly thrown back. Instinctively, his hands tightened on the rope. His outstretched arms felt they were being pulled from their sockets by the sudden shock. He was off balance and leaning off to Blue's right side. Clinging desperately to the reins and the neck rope, he used his legs to right himself. He pulled himself upright, barely getting a glimpse of Jan when they flashed past her. Finally, in a position of control, he pulled Blue down to an easy gallop, reining him toward Jan.

Jan's heart was beating rapidly and her breathing came in gulps. "My God, can **he** run!"

"Did you see? I nearly lost it, even with the neck rope," Bob said, smiling broadly. "Now you understand why the neck rope."

"Yes. God, what a thrill! I almost wet my pants," she exclaimed.

"Tsk...tsk...such a lady," he joked, laughing, and shaking his head. It was the first he'd heard her make that kind of statement. She was generally more reserved, but he knew it was her excitement talking.

"What was his time?" Bob asked, eagerly.

"Twenty-three seconds," she replied.

"Twenty three seconds," he repeated the number. "Not bad, considering my weight and not coming out of the gate clean.

Take a second or two off of that and you're looking at twenty-one, at best, and that isn't good enough," he added.

"Seems pretty darn fast to me," she said.

"If he's to have a chance at winning the futurity, his time has got to be about nineteen. I'll get him used to the gate--Stephan's weight would be about right," Bob said, as though he were talking to himself.

"He can do it. I know he can," Jan replied, enthusiasti-cally.

Bob looked at her beaming face. "I love your positive attitude, Jan. With you and Stephan in my corner, we're sure to win that race, come May."

"Are you going to take him out of the gate again?" Jan asked.

"Yep. But he needs about an hour or so of exercise to get him tired first."

"Why get him tired? I don't understand."

"Right now he wants to run. He's thinking about other things. Get him tired and he'll start paying attention to what we're trying to teach him."

"How do you know that?" she questioned.

"Tis a little thing called, experience," he returned.

"Oh, then you'd better get busy with him," she said, mounting Buck.

"Maybe so," he smiled.

When they reached the barn, Bob helped her off of Buck, capturing her in his arms. "You like doing this, don't you?"

"I love it," she said, then pressed her lips to his in a teasing kiss.

"I mean, helping me with Blue," he said, laughing.

"Yes, that too," she said, then giggled girlishly and kissed him again.

"This kind of horsing around could get to be a habit," he chuckled, gazing at her with appreciative eyes.

"I hope so," she said. "But you go horse around with Blue while I put something in the oven for dinner."

Bob watched her with admiration when she walked away toward the house, then he stepped up on Blue and pushed him back to the track.

THIRTEEN

While the days progressed, Blue's training became more rigorous. He now stood quietly in the starting gate, anticipating its sudden opening, and becoming oblivious to the sound of the gate slamming against its stop. His time for the quarter mile was running between 18.9 and 19.1 seconds, so he was ready, and all they had to do was keep him in shape.

On Saturday morning, the 10th of March, Stephan was excited, for this was the weekend he and Jan would be working together with Old Blue. When he entered Blue's stall and saw the bloodstained bedding, he anxiously inspected Blue for a wound on his body, then, seeing none, Stephan picked up his right front foot. The straw was stained where he stood. A nail had punctured the frog, the cushioning portion of his foot, and blood oozed out of the wound.

Bob and Jan were just entering the barn when Stephan ran to meet them. "Blue's **hurt**...hurt bad!" he shouted.

Jan looked at Bob with a concerned expression, then the three of them hurried to Blue's stall. Bob shoved the sliding stall door aside and saw Blue favoring his foot.

"Easy, boy," he said. He tapped his leg with the back of his hand. Blue picked up his foot and nickered softly. "Damn!" he exclaimed after inspecting the foot. He released the horse's foot, then stood up, placing his hands on his hips. His back was turned away from Jan and Stephan. He looked up at the ceiling and took a deep breath. In that moment, he saw all the years of work-- scraping and saving to acquire the right mare, breeding to the right stud to produce a horse colt that was born to run-- vanish overnight.

Jan and Stephan stepped up beside him. "How bad is it, Bob?" she asked.

He turned toward them. She was standing with her arm around Stephan. She could see the anguish and torment in his eyes and face. "Looks like he ran a nail up through the center of his foot. He'll never run with that kind of wound. It's going to take months to heal, and, by that time it'll be too late."

"We can fix it, Dad. It's two months till the race," Stephan said.

"Get me some blue vitriol, son. You know where it is. At least, we may be able to keep his foot from getting infected."

Stephan left the stall, and Bob moved the straw around with his foot, attempting to find what Blue had stepped on.

"Are you positive there's nothing that can be done for him?" Jan asked.

"Nothing short of a miracle. We may as well forget it. Quarter Horses drive with their front legs as well as their hind legs. They're not like Thoroughbreds. Even if it looked like it healed up okay, that right foot would still be too tender to get the speed out of him that we need to win," he concluded. He continued moving the straw, then his foot hit a solid object. He bent down and dug the object out of the straw. It was a short-splintered piece of wood, containing a sixteen-penny nail. He looked around the stall, then saw where it belonged. In the corner, a ribbed hay feeder was missing a partial rib. The feeder was built to allow a horse to pull hay between the ribs.

"That's where this came from," he said, pointing out the broken rib to Jan. "It busted off when he pulled hay out of the feeder."

Stephan entered the stall with the medicine and handed it to his father. He watched him dab the blue stuff on the horse's foot, then pour a small amount directly into the wound. He held his foot, for a minute, to allow the medicine to saturate it.

"We can pack his foot in mud, sometimes that helps." Stephan suggested. I can do it every day. Bet he'll be as good as new, come race day."

"I said to forget it, boy! It's over! He isn't ever going to run in a Futurity race," Bob said angrily, then hurriedly walked out of the stall.

Jan felt sorry for Bob, but his harsh words to Stephan made it seem that it was all his fault. She saw that Stephan was near tears. She reached out, putting her hand on his shoulder.

"He wasn't angry with you, dear. He's just upset. The big thing that he has hoped for is gone."

"But he just gave up on Blue! He isn't even goin' to try!"

"Well, your father knows horses pretty well. It's just one of those things we all have to accept. Let's go to the house. There's nothing more we can do for Blue right now."

"Yeah, okay," he said, dropping his head so the tears flowing freely, would not show, but Jan could feel his shoulders shuddering. Walking away, she glanced back at the beautiful black horse, feeling her own tears fall.

The snow was completely gone and the fields were responding to the warmth of the coming spring, with new growths of lush green grass carpeting them. Another month and a half and the cattle would be gone. Bob would receive approximately fifty-five hundred dollars for the wintering of them. He had been gambling on that money to carry them until the race. Winning the top prize money would have propelled him into the horse business. Breeders would have been clamoring for Blue's bloodline to be injected into their breeding programs. But, within an instant, those dreams were suddenly whisked away.

Jan and Stephan were subject to the impact of the situation, but Bob refused to talk about it, becoming quiet and distant. She could see the frustration mounting in him, and she became concerned that it would affect their relationship. She knew his feelings for her were held in reserve, and now she feared he might back away from her completely.

It was evening. Bob was tending to the horses and Stephan was doing his homework at the table. Jan had just finished cleaning up after the evening meal. Stephan looked up from his books and saw her putting on a light jacket.

"Whatcha gonna' do, Jan?" he asked.

"I thought I'd go out to the barn and see what your dad is up to," she replied, slipping on her boots.

"He's sure been actin' funny the last couple of days, hasn't he?"

She could see the worried expression on his face, but didn't know what to say or do to comfort him.

"He has a lot on his mind, honey. I'll see you in a little bit," she said, walking out the door.

She crept quietly into the horse barn, where the door to Blue's stall was open. Leaning against the opening with her arms folded, she watched while Bob treated the horse's foot. She remained silent until he had finished and stood up.

Bob became aware of her presence and looked down at her, but he said nothing. He turned his eyes away and gave Blue a pat on the neck.

"How's he doing?" she asked softly.

"His foot is hot and he's limping badly," he replied sullenly.

"There are other races, aren't there?" she asked gently, wrapping her arms around his waist.

"Sure, but none here that are worth more than the schooling he'd get. The big money is in California."

"Then let's enter him in the California races," she suggested, trying to be positive.

"Honey," he said, shaking his head, "that takes money and I just haven't got it. Racing Blue was just a dream anyway. I should have prepared myself better for something like this." He gently released her and slowly walked out of the barn. She couldn't help but feel saddened by his disheartened attitude.

The following morning, she tried to convince him to make a trip into town with her for supplies but he declined, telling her there were things he must do at the ranch, and that he also wanted to scout out some work.

Jan's eyes caught sight of a sign when she entered town, but she paid no immediate attention. Her intention was to get to the general store, then the sign suddenly registered in her mind. Stopping the pickup, she turned around and headed back toward it. It was the office of Lawrence Manning. After she parked the truck, she crossed the street to the office. When she walked in, she saw him sitting at his desk talking on the phone. He acknowledged her and motioned for her to take a seat. He appeared to her to be a man in his early seventies. His hair was snow white and thinning beyond his forehead. His face was weather-beaten from working outdoors.

After finishing his conversation, he looked at her questionably.

"You don't remember me, do you?" she asked.

"Ah...you do look a bit familiar," he responded, absently rubbing his chin.

"Bob Malloy introduced me to you, but it's been some time ago," she said, prompting his memory.

"Oh, yes, I remember now. Well, what can I do for you?"

Jan told him of the circumstances concerning Old Blue and the emotional effect it was having on Bob.

"A nail puncture in that area of the foot is a bad one. He's probably right. The foot wouldn't heal in time."

A feeling of dismay came over her. She had hoped this man could give her some magic cure that would speed up Blue's recovery in time for the race. Now it appeared she finally would have to accept the fact the horse would not be able to run.

"Then there isn't anything that can be done?" she asked in one last attempt.

Seeing the unhappy look on her face, Mister Manning leaned back in his chair. "I'm not sure. You see, the problem is, that wounds concerned with horses are notorious for healin' on the outside first, leavin' the interior of the wound to heal much slower. The trick is to keep the wound open and let it heal from the inside out. Salammoniac and vinegar is a good healer. You could soak his foot in a solution, but you need to pull the scabs off and keep the wound open."

"Could you write that down for me, and how you mix it. What is it exactly?" she asked excitedly, her mood beginning to lift again.

"It's a white, grainy powder; a kind of acid used in solderin'. The salammoniac eats away proud flesh, while the vinegar tends to heal," he explained.

"Can I get it at the general store?"

"That's the only place you can get it in this town," he replied, chuckling.

"Thank you, Mister Manning. I'd like to try this on the horse. If you should happen to see Bob, please don't tell him I'm treating Blue. I don't want to give him false hopes," she added.

He agreed to say nothing to Bob and cautioned her not to get her own hopes too high. However, his suggestion for treatment gave her renewed enthusiasm as she headed for the general store.

Jan later took Stephan into her confidence, telling him what she had learned from Lawrence Manning. Bob had managed to pick up some odd jobs from several of the ranchers in the area, and this gave her the opportunity to treat Blue. At times, when he had no work outside of the ranch, she managed to find things for him to do in the house, thus giving Stephan time to perform the treatments.

By the end of March, Blue was not limping. On one occasion she saddled Blue, wanting to see how he reacted to her weight. He carried her easily. She started putting him into short bursts of speed, then pulling him to a sudden stop.

She continued to treat the foot and exercise Blue. One day while working him inside the barn, she was surprised to see Lawrence Manning watching her. She brought Blue toward him and dismounted.

"I'm sorry, Mister Manning, I didn't see you come in. Have you been here long?" she asked pleasantly.

"Long enough to see that Old Blue is workin' pretty good."

"That solution you suggested worked very well. But you can still see the wound."

Lawrence picked up Blue's foot and brushed the dirt out of his hoof. He pressed on the frog and the sole. Blue never flinched a muscle. "I think you've done a good job, missy. I'd say, keep at it and he'll be runnin' in May."

"Oh, do you really think so! Bob will be so happy to hear that."

"Well, I wouldn't be tellin' him just yet. I'd give him a good stress test on that front foot first."

"You mean, test him out of the gate for a full distance."

"Yep. If he don't break down on the first run, I think he'll be okay."

"I'll get Stephan to help, the next time Bob's gone. I guess you know he isn't here. If he were, I wouldn't be working Blue," she said.

"Yep, I know it." He smiled. "I jimmied up my wife's television so's she couldn't watch them danged soap opries. Had her call him this mornin' ta come fix it."

Jan laughed. "You wanted to see how Blue was, didn't you?"

"Yep. Wanted to see if that salammoniac did the job. Blue's as fine a horse as I've ever seen. I'm glad that it's workin'."

"I'm so pleased that you came out to see him," she said warmly.

"I suppose you know I'll be takin' the cattle out soon. Thought I'd look 'em over while I was here."

"I think Blue has had enough for today. Why don't you come up to the house and have a cup of coffee before you do that?"

"No, I think I'll pass. That hobo coffee Bob makes drives my ticker crazy. But thank you for the offer."

"You are most welcome, Mister Manning," she said.

Jan was anxious to perform the stress test. She knew that Bob had agreed to wire a new maintenance shed for Chris Monford, and he was to start the job early Wednesday morning, so she talked Stephan into staying home from school that day so he could help her with Blue.

After Bob had left the ranch, she and Stephan set out to the barn. He hooked the starting gate to the tractor and pulled it into place. Jan strung the rope like Bob had done before. When all was ready, they prepared Blue for the test.

Backing him into the gate, Jan closed the door, then she took her place at the far end of the track. Stephan set Blue. He was nervously anticipating and praying that his foot would hold up. But his prayers, for the most part, were for Bob, for he knew how depressed he had been. He gripped the reins and the neck rope, waiting for that moment when the gate would spring open.

The moment he placed the racing saddle on Blue, the horse sensed something was going to happen, so he arched his neck and raised his tail, prancing proudly to the starting gate. He could feel the tautness of his body transmit his energy into Stephan's senses, and horse and rider became one entity.

Stephan raised his arm, then swung it downward. The rope tripped the latch holding the door. Blue had not forgotten the familiar click of the latch, and he lunged forward when the door slammed against its stop. Stephan leaned low and forward over his withers. He gripped the rope tightly, keeping the reins loose to give Blue his head. The track became a blur when he pulled ground beneath him with his driving, ever-reaching front legs. His hindquarters pushed him with seemingly relentless power.

Passing Jan, he made a wide turn and brought Blue down to his prancing walk. "What was his time?" he asked, approaching Jan.

"Twenty-point-nine," she replied excitedly. "And that, is going to make your father **very** happy!" she exclaimed.

Slipping to the ground, Stephan asked, "Do you want to cool him out?"

"You bet," she said, jumping onto the saddle.

Stephan's mind contained a sense of triumph. He had overcome the barrier between Jan and felt that, finally, he had come to love her. And now, the latest of those triumphs was Blue. Barring further accidents, he would run in the Futurity. He tried to imagine Bob's reaction when he learned what he and Jan had accomplished, thanks to the advise of Lawrence Manning.

FOURTEEN

She wanted to surprise Bob, and also wanted Stephan present when she did, cautioning him not to say anything to his father. Stephan already had missed one day of school, so the special event would have to wait until the weekend.

Stephan brought Blue into the horse barn. They worked together; one currying him and the other pulling his tail, removing the knots from it. They talked excitedly about Blue's chances of winning the Futurity, but according to Stephan's enthusiasm, he already had won it.

After pulling the starting gate into the place where Bob had dropped it previously, they parked the tractor, then walked to the house. The two of them had grown very close in the passing weeks, and Jan felt Stephan was her own son. She smiled, realizing how like his father he was. Stubborn and prideful, but also sensitive and kind.

The problems they had encountered since her arrival were overwhelming, and they had overcome them together. Yet, the biggest problem of all still remained, at least to Bob. If it were up to her, she could remain Jan forever. Why couldn't he see that, if no one had come in search of her after this much time had passed, then no one ever would?

She fixed Stephan a plate of cookies, letting him have his coffee, but laced heavily with milk.

"Do you have any idea about how we could surprise Dad?" he asked.

"Well, I thought you could set the starting gate on the track, then saddle up Blue and have him out there. Then I'll bring your father out to the track. Can you do that?"

"Sure, but how are you goin' to keep him from the barn?"

"I'm sure I can think of something to keep him in the house."

"Yeah...I guess so," Stephan allowed, hesitantly, pondering the situation. Then his eyes widened when he looked at her, and suddenly he broke into a broad smile.

She looked at his smiling face a moment, then her cheeks turned bright red. "Stephan!" she exclaimed, her voice admonishing. But her lips parted in a half-smile, knowing what was tripping through his mind. "I'm surprised at you." Her tone caused Stephan's cheeks to flush. They stood laughing at each other's embarrassment.

For Jan and Stephan the next two days were filled with anticipation of the coming weekend.

But the depression Bob felt had not yet left his mind. He could not understand their light-hearted attitude when they joked and playfully teased each other. They tried to include him in their fun-loving antics, but he remained quiet.

On Saturday morning, Bob could smell the aroma of pancakes cooking when he strode to the table and sat down. Jan set a piping hot cup of coffee in front of him, then greeted him with a warm kiss.

"Isn't Stephan having any breakfast?" he asked, noticing the boy was already gone.

"He's out feeding the horses. I'll fix him something when he comes in."

"You know, I haven't said much about this, but I'm glad to see that you and he are getting along so well," Bob said, gazing into her cheerful face.

"Things have a way of working out. I'm just glad they worked out favorably."

"Well, some things do, I guess," he returned, somberly.

She knew what his statement was in reference to, but let it pass without comment and returned to the kitchen. He sipped at his coffee, watching her, thinking how much he loved her. She was the only bright spot in his life other than Stephan. Blue was a great disappointment, and it had taken a lot out of him. He tried to conceive the loss of this woman, should she be married and have children, but his mind could not picture himself without her, yet it was a possibility they both had to face.

Bob knew that she loved him, and even though she had said that her senses told her there was no commitment to anyone, they couldn't be sure. He was engrossed in his thoughts when Jan brought their breakfast to the table.

She waved her hand in front of him. "Hello in there," she said, smiling at him. "You look like you're a million miles away."

"I'm sorry," he said, shaking his head, "I guess my mind's been drifting a lot lately."

They ate in silence. Jan was trying to figure out how she could keep him in the house longer. She wanted to give Stephan time enough to do his part, but, before she knew it, Bob had finished eating and was downing the last of his coffee.

Rising from the table, he reached for his coat. "I'd better give Stephan a hand with the horses."

"Ah...can you do me a favor first? I want to wash the curtains and was wondering if you would take them down for me?"

"Why? They don't look dirty to me."

"Well, they collect dust even if they do look clean. Get me the ones in your room, too," she ordered.

While Bob set about taking the curtains down, Jan breathed a sigh of relief that he hadn't argued further.

"Thank you," she said, when he handed them to her. Then Bob put on his coat and was ready to leave the house again.

"Wait for me. I'll go out with you," she said, casting the curtains aside.

"I thought you wanted to wash those."

"I do, but they can wait for a while."

He shook his head. "Then why did you have to have them down now?"

"I just wanted to have them ready to wash. Give me a minute to comb my hair," she said, going into the bathroom.

"What do you have to comb your hair for? You're only going out to the barn. Are you afraid you'll scare the horses?" He laughed.

Ten minutes passed. Bob was sitting at the table, impatiently drumming his fingers, when she came out of the bathroom. "Is there anything else you need to do before we get to the barn?"

She smiled sweetly at him. "No. Are you ready to go?"

"I was ready half an hour ago."

"I haven't held you up that long," she replied.

"Women...they got no conception of time." He chuckled, opening the door for her.

"It sounds good to hear you laugh. You haven't done that in quite some time," she said, slipping her arm into his.

"Not much to laugh about lately," he said somberly.

Jan suddenly stopped and looked into his sober face. "Bob, there's a lot to be happy about. I love you, and I hope you still love me. I know Stephan likes me now, so we have a lot to be happy about."

"I could never stop loving you," he said, gazing down at her uptilted face.

"I hope not, darling. Now come with me, I want to show you something."

She led him past the corner of the large barn and beyond the corral where the cattle had spent the snowy days of winter. When the track came into view, he saw Stephan holding Blue's reins at the starting gate.

Bob's expression reflected genuine surprise, when he saw Blue prancing around Stephan, his tail held high and his head up. He felt a moment of exhilaration flow through his body. Blue didn't show the slightest sign of limping. However, surmising their intentions, his feeling of joy was short-lived.

"Why are you doing this, Jan? He can't run on that foot. He couldn't take the pressure, I've told you that." His voice was strained.

"He can run. Stephan and I have been treating his foot. He quit limping, and two days ago...we **ran** him."

"You raced him a full four hundred-forty yards?" He was surprised and a little irritated that they had done this on their own without informing him.

"Yes, and he was wonderful! It didn't bother him a bit."

"I don't understand. How? What kind of treatment?"

"Lawrence Manning told me what to do. Even he wasn't sure it would work, but it did. Come on, I'll show you," she said, pulling him toward Stephan and Blue.

Bob reached out and grabbed her by the arm. "Hold on just a darn minute! I want to know what kind of treatment you're talking about. What'd he tell you?"

"He told me about a mixture of salammoniac and vinegar, and something about proud flesh and I don't know what all. He even came out to see if it was working," she went on excitedly.

"Well, I'll be damned," Bob said. "I'd given up all hopes, but if Lawrence told you what to do, then I guess it must be all right."

Stephan was smiling wildly when they approached him. "Dad, he ran good! Look at him, he wants to run now!" he yelled exuberantly.

"Easy, son. Hold him still. I want to look at that foot." Bob cradled Blue's foot between his knees. He felt the hoof and sole for heat; there was none. Then he pressed on his sole and frog and didn't detect any tenderness. He set his foot free and stood up, turning toward Stephan.

"Did you time him?"

"Twenty-point-nine," Stephan informed him proudly.

"Twenty-point-nine." His voice was not audible and his lips barely moved as he repeated the time to himself. He hesitated for a moment, then said, "Put him in the gate!"

"Do you want to ride him for your father, Stephan?" Jan asked.

Stephan looked at her, then at his father. "Yep, do you mind, Dad?"

"Go ahead, son."

Blue's time was even better than it had been two days earlier, by several tenths of a second. He dismounted and started to lead Blue back to where Bob and Jan were waiting for him. Bob bodily picked Jan up and swung her around.

She could see the life come back into his eyes. He smiled at her, and then kissed her full on the mouth.

Stephan stood with Blue, watching them with a big grin on his face. When Bob finally released Jan, he walked up to Stephan and hugged him. He even gave the horse a quick hug. Bob looked at the two people he loved most in the world, the pride and emotion overwhelming him.

From that Saturday morning until the weekend before the race, Blue's training took place at precisely the same time every day. He was worked methodically against another horse. Hours were spent working him out of the gate, sharpening his anticipation of its sudden opening for clean explosive starts. He also received daily rubdowns, particularly his legs.

Bob was pleased with Blue's progress. He was running triple-A, and getting stronger each time they worked him. He purposely delayed making arrangements for a jockey, wanting to see if Blue would remain sound throughout his conditioning. Satisfied with his continued progress, he made contact with a local jockey who had run many backyard races.

Lenny Chase was the man's name. He was in his forties and slim built. Jan was unimpressed by his appearance. Lenny was unshaven, dressed shabbily, and his personal hygiene left much to be desired. He supposedly could ride, and came to the ranch in the latter stages of training to get a feel for the way Blue handled, and to learn if he had any particular quirks.

Lenny worked Blue out of the gate six times over a period of two weeks, and he was impressed with Blue's natural, smooth, running ability. He agreed to ride for Bob, and they signed a contract to that effect. He said he would meet them at Yakima Meadows on Saturday, the weekend of the race.

Stephan expressed his own desires to ride Blue, but Bob would not hear of it, saying it was too dangerous and he was too inexperienced. Reluctantly, he abided by his decision.

"I guess you know what you're doing," she said, feeling sorry for Stephan, then added, "But he's so cocksure of himself, I wonder if Lenny's as good as he thinks he is?"

"Lenny's good, Jan. There's more to running a race than just pointing the horse down the track. He's track wise. He knows what to look for and how to avoid getting blocked or hooked.

Stephan doesn't have that kind of experience, and I don't want to take a chance on him getting hurt."

"Well, I hope he doesn't live up to his name."

"What do you mean live up to his name?"

"Chasing the horses to the finish line instead of leading them."

The weekend of the big race had finally come. It would be a weekend filled with excitement, great expectations, and also apprehension. Blue was ready, his legs were sound, and physically his muscles were tuned to perfection. He nickered softly when Bob loaded him into the horse trailer. He knew he was being prepared for some big event.

At six-thirty Bob closed and latched the tailgate of the trailer. Jan and Stephan carried out two suitcases and placed them in the back end of the pickup.

"Are we all set?" Bob asked, climbing into the truck.

"Yes. I packed us a lunch, and the doors to the house are locked, so we're ready to hit the road," Jan announced jovially.

The trip to Yakima from the ranch would take four hours, and Jan was in awe of the scenery, particularly of Glacial Lake Chalan and the drive along the Columbia River. They exited the freeway at the Yakima Avenue exit, which was the main street through town. When he saw the Chinook Motel, Bob pulled the pickup over to the curb. It was an elaborate-looking place, and he felt Jan deserved the luxury it presented. He acquired two rooms, then they drove to Yakima Meadows and registered Blue for the Futurity.

A stall was secured for Blue, and Bob drove the pickup to the designated stall. The rest of the afternoon was spent preparing what would be Blue's living quarters for the next two days, and the stable was abuzz with people bringing in horses from all over the country for the two-day event.

Jan, Bob and Stephan enjoyed the activity. The three of them walked through the stall area, viewing the competition that Blue would have to face and visiting with other hopefuls.

After eating a late dinner at the motel, they walked to their rooms. Stephan took his father's key and ran ahead; he wanted to watch television.

Bob stopped at Jan's room. She unlocked the door and swung it open. "Want to come in for a while?" she asked.

"Yes, I want to, but...."

"I know," she said and smiled sadly.

"Hey, now. What kind of a look is that?" he asked, seeing her saddened expression. "Tomorrow may be the day." He was thinking positively about the race.

"I'm not worried about the race. I know Blue will win. I was thinking about the deal we made, that after the race I could leave," she said.

"Jan, you're not going anywhere!" he replied sternly. "That was a long time ago, and things have changed. Besides, where would you go?"

She looked up at him with tears in her eyes. "I was hoping you'd say something like that, because I don't want to leave...I never did. I only threatened to leave, to see if you felt about me the way I felt about you."

Bob tilted her face up and gently wiped the tears away with the back of his hand.

"Women. As long as I live, I'll never understand you creatures." He drew her close, and their lips touched in a lingering kiss.

When they parted he said, "I'll see you in the morning. Lenny is supposed to be in early, and I'd like to go out to the track and talk to him before we have breakfast."

It had been a long day for everyone, so when Bob entered their room, he found Stephan sound asleep. He didn't wake him, just covered him with a blanket.

He was tired, but too filled with excitement to sleep. He started thinking about Blue and the race. He wanted the horse to win, not only for the financial gain but also for the woman and son he cherished.

He smiled when he thought of Jan remembering that silly deal they had made. He had completely forgotten about it. She'd been with him nearly nine months, with no sign of recovering her memory, and it was possible she never would. There were no reports in the newspapers or the electronic media of anyone fitting her description missing.

His heart was telling him they had become a family, and to marry her. But his mind cautioned him against such an action, rationalizing the devastating effects should she suddenly regain her memory.

It was then he decided to compromise with his thoughts and feelings. The three of them would go to Seattle after the race. He'd always thought she probably came from a large city. If Seattle was her city, there may be something familiar about it to spark her memory. If not, then at least he had tried, and they would return to the ranch and put her memory loss behind them.

A sudden chill caused him to shutter when he thought of the possibility that something in Seattle would trigger her memory. He loved her and didn't want to lose her, but she had a life before and he must accept whatever it contained. The thought of losing her tore at his heart. If she regained her memory, it would be impossible for her to consider the relationship that had linked them together under the influence of her amnesia. That part of their lives would live only in their memories.

Monday could be the beginning of the end of their lives together. He stretched out on the bed, hoping sleep would overcome him, but the thoughts pouring through his mind did not allow him that luxury.

FIFTEEN

Post time was set for one-thirty, Sunday afternoon, and Bob was cleaning Blue's stall when Lenny appeared. He told him the position they had drawn, but he seemed indifferent to the news.

"I can see you're really deelighted about the draw," Lenny said sarcastically.

"Of course, I am. I'm just not letting myself get caught up in false hopes," Bob said, attempting to explain away his lack of interest.

"Well, bein' as how we got the tenth position, and the way Blue has worked out of the gate, I figure we can get a jump on the rest of 'em. Plus bein' tenth, and on the outside, there's no way to get boxed," Lenny continued.

"Lenny, I'm sure you'll run the best race you can," Bob said, while pitching the last of the old bedding outside.

"Yes, sir, you got yourself quite a horse here. I don't think he's gonna' have any trouble winnin' that race," Lenny rambled on.

Bob walked out of the stall and jabbed the fork tines into the dirt of the breezeway. "I'll meet you back here before post time, Lenny. I've got to pick up Stephan and Jan," he said, walking away.

Lenny turned to Blue. "Seems like he's lost all interest in this race, Blue. Maybe he's just worried you won't win. Well, you and me are gonna' show 'em how to win a race, boy. Maybe that'll perk him up." Blue nickered and twitched his ears.

At eight o'clock Bob got back to the motel and picked up Stephan and Jan. They had breakfast, then headed for the track. Bob parked the pickup, then Stephan hurriedly jumped out, saying he was going to the barn to see Blue. In an instant, he was out of sight, leaving Jan and Bob to themselves.

She took his hand into hers. Their eyes met and held to each other. They seemed to know each other's thoughts. "I love you, Jan," he said softly.

"And I love you," she replied, snuggling in his arms.

He pressed his lips upon her cheek. "I thought we'd spend a few days in Seattle after the race. Would you like that?"

"Hey," she replied cheerfully, "that would be great, but expensive."

"Hang the expense. You've worked hard and gotten little out of it. You deserve a vacation. We can handle a couple of days to relax and enjoy ourselves. There's the Pike Place Market, the Seattle Center, and Woodland Park Zoo. Stephan's never seen any of those things, and I think you'd like it, too."

"I'd like it anywhere, as long as you were there."

He hugged her lovingly. Tilting her head, he looked at her a moment, and their lips met in a kiss. She felt his trembling hands cupping her face.

"Are you all right, Bob?" She asked, with concern in her voice.

"Yes, I'm fine. Why?"

"Well, you're shaking. I've never felt you tremble so." He looked down at her positive, sunny face, and it almost broke his heart. "Oh, it's just that you excite me so much."

"Hmmm, then I like it," she purred.

"I do, too, but I think we should mosey over to the barn."

"Why? Are you having a problem?" she asked, pursing her lips.

"Not yet," he replied with a half grin, then climbed out of the pickup. "Come on, hon, let's find Stephan."

When Bob and Jan walked up, they found Lenny dressed in his riding togs, sitting on a bale of straw while Stephan put the final touches to Blue with the curry brush.

"Any last words of wisdom before Blue hits the track?" Lenny drawled.

"Win, Lenny. Just win," Bob said, patting Blue on the back.

Lenny opened the stall door and Stephan led Blue into the breezeway. Bob assisted in getting Blue ready, cinching the saddle in place, and then boosting Lenny onto the horse.

"We never used a bat on him, Lenny. He's always ran his best for us without it, but use your own discretion."

"I'll get as much out of him as I can. See you in the winner's circle," Lenny chirped with a big smile.

They watched Lenny leave the stall area for the track. "Do you think Blue can win, Dad?"

"You heard Lenny. He said he would see us in the winner's circle. If Old Blue runs like he did in his trials, we got better than a fifty-fifty chance of winning."

"Come on, you two, we'd better find a place to watch the race," Jan urged.

The horses were already at the starting gate, when they got to their seats. The gate handler worked his way down the line, latching each gate. After the horses were settled, Old Blue didn't exhibit any excited concern. He appeared calm, only the twitch of an ear. His eyes were looking straight ahead, but Lenny could feel the tension of his muscles coil, anticipating the gate opening.

Lenny sat with knees high and his weight over Blue's shoulder. Then suddenly came the loud clang of the bell. Lenny felt his boot tick the gate when Blue leaped at the ringing sound.

His powerful forearms dug deep into the soft, sandy dirt of the track, and his hind legs sprayed the dirt high in the air behind him. He was a half length ahead of the pack. Five seconds into the race, Lenny cut Blue across the pack. He wanted inside close to the rail. A horse and rider had taken the outside position, gaining rapidly on Blue. Another horse was on the inside. Both were challenging, and close. Did they mean to attempt to block him in? He waited another second or two. They could block or hook a stirrup if they got too close, possibly costing Blue the race. Lenny raised the bat; he could wait no longer. He brought it down squarely across Blue's right hindquarter. Lenny felt Blue drop beneath him, then felt a sudden acceleration he didn't think possible. The rushing wind grabbed at the loose material in the sleeves of his riding jacket, making a fluttering sound. In an instant the two horses beside him were suddenly a length behind him. He watched the finish line fast approaching. "Only a second or two more, Blue!" Lenny's heart pounded with excitement, for never had he ridden such a magnificent animal! Then, Blue backed off gently, the finish line just yards away, and Pat's Pride won the race by a head.

Lenny jumped off Blue in a hurry. He saw blood on the right foot and picked it up. The old wound was opened again.

Stephan shouted encouraging words at Blue, while Jan held her breath and squeezed Bob's arm. Bob took a deep breath, but he knew Lenny had sensed the same thing, and saw Lenny's arm raise the bat. Jan screamed with excitement when she saw Blue cross the finish line, and Bob put his arm around her.

"I saw him finish first," Jan said.

"Did you see Blue, Dad. Do you think that he won?" Stephan asked.

Bob looked at them and took a deep breath. "We lost. Something's happen. We've got to get back to the stall."

Lenny was rubbing down Old Blue's legs. When the three approached him, Lenny looked up, saw them and stood up. He had a sad look on his face. "I was sure we had that one in the bag. Look at your horse."

Bob took the right foot and held it up. Lenny had cleaned the blood off the sole and the frog. There was still a slight trickle of blood around the sole.

"I shouldn't have used the bat. When I did, the horse took off, and that's when I noticed him flinch. I'm sorry, Bob," Lenny said.

Bob put the foot down and stood up. "You win a little and lose a little, but it was close," Bob noted.

"Stephan can walk him. I've got to go and check my ride back to Winthrop."

"Okay," they shook hands and Bob said, "I left your check at the office."

"Thanks, Bob."

Stephan walked Old Blue around the paddock area while Bob put new bedding in the stall. Four men were looking at Blue when Jan walked up to them.

"I think he's a wonderful animal," Jan said.

They turned around, and one man spoke. "Do you own this horse?"

"No, Bob Malloy is the owner. Would you like to talk to him"He's right there." She pointed at the stall.

Bob was finished and hung the pitch fork up on the wall when the four men approached.

Jan sat on a bale of straw, while the four men introduced themselves to Bob. They were all dressed in western gear.

"I'm Larry." He introduced himself then pointed out the rest. "This is Stu, Mark and Rick. That horse is one beautiful animal. If the rider would have used the bat earlier, he would have won."

"I know, but...."

"You want to sell him," Larry interrupted.

"**NO,** I wouldn't do that. It's because he used the bat, that's why he lost. He stepped on a nail a month ago, and it had healed nicely. But when the jockey used the bat it opened the wound again."

Larry picked up the right foot. "Stepped on a nail, huh." He put the foot down and extended his right arm to touch the horse and walked around it.

"Who's he by?" Stu asked.

"Three Bar out of a King mare," Bob answered.

"He's run the futurity and I...we all think he would have won."

"He would have," Bob confirmed."

The men gathered at the paddock fence and talked a little. Then Larry came forward and spoke to Bob. "Where you from?"

"I have a ranch in Winthrop," Bob said.

"Why don't you turn your ranch into a stud farm. We got twenty head among the four of us. We'll pay five hundred dollars per head, and pay for the mares until their settled, how's that?"

Bob didn't show any emotion. "That's fine. If you will give me your addresses, I'll fill out a form and send it to all of you."

173

Glancing at and Jan and Stephan, he could see their eyes wide with excitement.

They all had cards with their name and address upon them. nd When they left and were out of sight, the three of them went wild.

Bob had a feeling of well-being. In effect, his dreams . had actually come true even though blue hadn't won the race. His mind reeled with thoughts of good times ahead financially. Eventually he would be in control of his own destiny, upgrading his own stock and, through selective breeding, producing triple-A running horses.

Bob gathered Jan and Stephan into his arms. "You know, if it hadn't been for the two of you, this day would not have existed for me."

"Don't forget Mister Manning...he told me what to do," Jan reminded.

"Why didn't you let me know what the two of you were doing?"

"We didn't want you to be disappointed if the treatments didn't work," she replied.

He hugged both of them tightly against him. "You guys have become quite a team."

"I think we all make a good team," Jan bragged.

Her statement that they made a good team, turned Bob's thoughts to Seattle. It brought the weight of fear that she would recognize something in the city to spur her memory. The possibility was remote, but still disturbing. If that occurred, most likely there wouldn't be a threesome team, only Stephan and himself.

"That's right, Jan, we are a good team. Hey...what are we doing standing around here? I could go for a big, thick, juicy steak," he said, feigning enthusiasm to cover up the deepening thoughts within himself.

"I'm for that," Stephan said and Jan agreed. After making sure Blue was taken care of, the three of them headed into town.

The next day Bob awoke to the sounds of the television playing. He lay still a moment rubbing his eyes, then popped out of bed and showered. When he reentered the room to dress, he saw Stephan still glued to the television set.

"Better turn that thing off and get yourself ready to go, son."

"I'm ready. All I got to do is put on a shirt and my shoes."

"And comb that hair," Bob said, stuffing his shirt into his jeans. He put the finishing touches to himself, then heard a soft rap at the door.

When he opened the door, Jan stood there. "I thought I'd better see what happened to you two. You know it's almost eleven o'clock," she said, stepping inside.

"Come on, Stephan, they quit serving breakfast at eleven-thirty. Are you ready to eat, Jan?" Bob asked.

"I'm starved," she replied.

After breakfast, Bob suggested Jan pack up their belongings while he made arrangements for the care of Old Blue for the few days they were in Seattle.

Nearing Seattle, Bob exited the freeway at 188th, then to highway 99 and the SeaTac Air Terminal complex.

"I thought we'd stop at the Red Lion, get a couple of rooms, and stoke up on some food."

"The Red Lion sounds like an expensive place," Jan said.

"I feel like splurging. I think we've earned it."

They entered the Red Lion lobby, secured two rooms, then proceeded to the restaurant. Stephan was in awe of the dining room. He'd never seen tables covered with white linen and lighted candles on them. His boots sunk into the plush carpeting when the hostess led them to their table.

"Boy, dad," he said in subdued tones, "this is sure ritzy! I bet it costs a lot of money to eat here."

Bob smiled, then glanced at Jan. "Maybe so, but you don't worry about that, son."

"I saw a swimmin' pool when we came in. Can anybody swim in it?"

"I suppose so, as long as their staying here, but you don't have a suit."

"Perhaps we can get you a suit tomorrow," Jan suggested.

"Boy, that would be neat. Ain't never swum in a real pool before."

"You never swam in a real pool," Jan corrected.

"Yeah, I know. That's what I just said."

They ordered their meal, and while waiting to be served, their conversation centered around the past events of the race. Bob talked of the plans he had for the ranch, but when their meal arrived, he ate in silence.

A part of his dream had just been fulfilled. But the most important part, still a dream, was Jan. He wanted her with him because she had become so much a part of his life. Yet, he had to know what her life had been. His mind hoped Seattle would bring her memory back, but his heart wished the opposite.

"A penny for your thoughts."

Shaken from those thoughts, he looked up. "Oh, I was just thinking of what we could do tomorrow."

"You said something about a farmer's market, that could be interesting," Jan suggested.

"There's lots of things to see here. I guess the market is a good place to start. We may even get a bathing suit for the both of you."

"Don't leave yourself out. If one of us goes swimming, we all go," she said, smiling.

At ten o'clock the next morning, they entered the Pike Place Market. Foot traffic was heavy, and people made purchases of fresh vegetables and fruits. Further down the aisle, they watched the fish vendors take an order, then expertly throw the fish to a colleague who wrapped it.

The three watched, fascinated and entertained by the chatter of the vendors and their customers. Moving on, they entered an area containing individual shops. One was only limited by imagination to the variety of wares available here.

"I was here once, years ago," Bob said. "Things have changed a bit, but there used to be a good pie shop. I wonder if it's still around?"

"Could be. Stephan, keep your eyes open for a pie shop," Jan said, laughing.

They wandered in and out of the shops, occasionally making a purchase of some unique trinket, a memento, and even bought themselves some new clothes, along with their bathing suits. Sidewalk minstrels with guitars, banjos, and some odd-looking instruments lined the cobblestone street. They played their melodic tunes, in the hope of collecting coins for their efforts from those who passed by.

Stephan, become entranced with the varied cultures gathered in this place, strange people with strange instruments playing strange music. They walked through the market, he was taken by the visible ethnicity of the people he saw.

"There sure are a lot of strange people in here."

Bob heard his statement, and placed his hand on his shoulder. "They're people just like us, Stephan. Some are probably from other countries. They dress differently, so they look kind of strange. See that man with the big bushy beard wearing a turban. Well, he's probably from the Middle East. If you were in his country, dressed as you are, **you** would look strange."

"Yeah, I guess so. I never thought of it like that."

While Bob and Stephan were talking, Jan saw a wine shop. Getting Bob's attention, they crossed the street and entered the shop. Several people were gathered around a table. Behind it, the proprietor was describing the various wines set upon the table for tasting. He poured small amounts of wine into dixie cups and passed them out.

The group of people finally thinned, and Bob and Jan moved forward. After several sips of the different wines, they found a bottle they liked. The man called out the brand of wine, then said, "You can pick up your purchase at the cashier's check stand."

The line was moving slow. "I wish that woman would hurry up. She must be buying out the store," Bob said quietly.

"Shush, she'll hear you," Jan returned.

The woman signed an invoice and slipped it into her purse. When she started to walk away, she glanced at Jan, then suddenly stopped. Her gaze held fast to Jan's face for a moment.

Then she smiled and said, "I'm sorry for staring. You just look so much like someone I knew."

Bob saw the partially startled look on the woman's face and put his arm around Jan. "Who did you think she was?"

"No one. I'm sorry, I was mistaken. The person...has passed away," she said, then briskly left the shop.

Bob and Jan looked into each other's eyes. "She thought she knew me."

"She also said, whoever you reminded her of was dead." He could feel her trembling body and kept his arm around her. She stared, almost mesmerized.

"Jan, are you okay?" She heard his voice intermingled with her thoughts. She looked up at him and shook her head. "Yes, yes, I'm fine."

The line moved closer to the check stand. "Look, Jan, why don't you grab a seat by Stephan while I pick up our stuff."

The cashier called out his wine and the price of fifteen dollars. Bob dipped into his pocket and pulled out the cash.

"Do you know who that woman was, three or four customers ahead of me?" he asked.

"I don't keep track of the women that come in here."

"She signed an invoice. You have the copy right there on your spindle."

"What do you want with her?"

"I think I know her."

The cashier looked at the invoice for a moment. "She works at the Ramada Inn, manager, I think. She can tell you her name, if she's a mind to."

"Thanks," Bob said and walked away.

Another hour was spent in the market, with no sign of a pie shop.

"Do you want to go back to the motel or drive around for awhile?"

"Let's go back to the motel. We can go swimmin'," Stephan said.

"Sounds good to me," Jan agreed.

Back in their room Stephan slipped into his new bathing suit, but Bob made no attempt to change into his.

"Ain't you gonna' swim with us, Dad."

"Yeah, but not right now. You go ahead with Jan. I'll be down shortly."

"Why don't you come with us now?"

"Well, son, I want our stay in Seattle to be kind of special for Jan. I'm depending on you to keep her busy while I get some flowers for her room."

"Yeah, women like that kind of stuff, don't they?"

"I think they do, and it's fun doing it. Now don't you let her know what's going on."

"I won't, I promise. I'll go get her now and take her to the pool."

Bob waited until Stephan and Jan had left, then he slipped out of the room, and took the elevator to the parking area. He pulled his pickup into the Ramada Inn and walked into the lobby.

He surveyed the room, looking for the woman he'd seen in the market. Not seeing her, he stepped up to the desk.

"I'd like to see the manager, please," he said.

"Who should I say is calling?" the clerk asked.

"Bob Malloy, but we've never met."

The clerk eyed him for a moment, deciding whether or not to honor the request. "I'll see if she's in," he said, then disappeared into a room behind the desk.

Moments passed and soon a woman appeared from the room and stood at the counter...the same woman he'd seen in the wine shop.

"Yes, you wanted to talk with me?"

"Yes, miss. We met briefly at the wine shop. Do you remember?"

"Yes, I remember you and the woman with you. What a shock to see someone who looked so much like my friend,"

"You said this friend of yours died. Tell me about her."

"Look, Mister--"

"Malloy, Bob Malloy."

"Mister Malloy...I don't know what your interest is. I was simply caught off guard by the lady with you."

"Please, miss, it's very important. I saw your expression when you looked at my friend. That's why I have to talk to you. Is there some place we can talk more privately?"

The woman looked at him straight on. She saw the deep concern in his eyes. "I'm Patricia Duncan, Mister Malloy. Let's go into the dining room."

She led him to a booth away from the other patrons.

"Could you please tell me what this is all about?"

"Well, several months ago I found the woman you saw me with, wandering around in some really desolate country near Winthrop. She was in pretty bad shape..."

"Mister Malloy, I don't see what that has to do..."

"She lost her memory, Miss Duncan. She can't remember anything of her past, who she is, where she came from, nothing. We've had fingerprint searches made by AVIS and the FBI. They've found nothing."

"And you think...you can't be serious. I told you my friend is dead. She died in a terrible car accident."

"I know that's what you said, but you thought you knew her, so much so that you were shocked. You looked like you had seen a ghost."

Patricia stared into the distance, concentrating on Jan's image. She turned her gaze to Bob. "The similarity is so striking. Melissa Cory, that was her name, like your friend, had a small scar just above her left eyebrow, in the same identical spot. That's what caught my attention first, and she does look a lot like Melissa, but being the same woman is impossible."

"Did you attend this...Melissa's funeral?"

"Oh no, she's from New York...just a memorial service. Look, Mister Malloy, she was here for a writer's conference for a few days, then left for Spokane for another conference. Her business manager, Mister Justin, called here, checking on her. He must have had her itinerary because she was to return here, turn in the car she rented, and catch her flight back to New York the following day. He was quite worried about her because she never got to Spokane. Several days later he called again and said that Melissa had been killed in an auto accident, in Idaho. It struck me as being strange."

"Because she was supposed to be in Spokane," Bob interjected.

"Yes, just over the weekend."

"You say, writer's conference, an author?"

"No, she was a publisher. She was the sole owner of the Dove Publishing Company." Patricia signaled a waitress to bring them some coffee, then turned her attention back to him. "I'm afraid I'm not much help...."

The memorial service nagged at Bob. It meant the body of the woman was not present at the service, and he could not erase the image of Patricia's expression when seeing Jan. He sipped at his coffee. Perhaps it was coincidence that Jan had a scar identical to the woman called Melissa. There was another question he had to ask. "Miss Duncan, the car accident, when did it happen?"

She hesitated a moment, thinking. "It was last year, yes...in late August."

A sudden sensation penetrated his stomach when he listened to the answer; that put the accident in the same time frame he'd found Jan. Patricia's shocked expression when seeing Jan, the identical scar, it just seemed too circumstantial to him. He sipped at his coffee again, wetting a dry spot in his throat. `Doctor Wooward was right...Melissa Cory,' he thought. "Miss Duncan, Jan...may be Melissa Cory."

"Impossible...I just can't believe it."

"You thought you knew her. Look at the coincidences. No body at the services, the scar, and the time of the accident is very close to when I found her," Bob explained.

"It's crazy, Mister Malloy," she said. She recalled Carl Justin's description of the accident. He'd said the car had exploded, and there wasn't much left of anything, but the occupant was a woman. A portion of the engine was found containing the serial number which led to the auto rental agency, and to Melissa Cory. Yet what Bob was telling her had some validity. Was it possible? she wondered.

"I know it sounds crazy, but if--"

Patricia interrupted him. "I can see where you're coming from, Bob. But if your friend **is** Melissa, then who was the woman in the car, and how did she get it?"

"All I know is what I've told you. It's enough to make me wonder, and you can help. If you could talk to her about the conference, anything you can remember that you might have talked about, if she is this...Miss Cory, it may jog her memory."

She looked into his anxious eyes and studied them for a moment. "Your friend, Jan...you're in love with her, aren't you?"

He lowered his eyes. "Yes, I love her very much."

"When do you want me to talk to her."

"I'll bring her in for dinner tonight."

SIXTEEN

Bob stepped out on the small balcony of his room and stared down at the pool. He watched Jan and Stephan playing in the water, his mind recalling what Patricia had told him, that Melissa Cory was the sole owner of the Dove Publishing Company. That statement implied wealth, and wealth had other implications attached to it, lavish parties, the opera and perhaps the ballet.

All these things conjured up images in his mind that he couldn't relate to any more, or even cared about. It was not difficult for him to see Jan in that role. She was intelligent.

He felt a sudden emptiness surround him. He'd wanted to give up the idea that she may see something that would plunge her back in time, but it was too late for that now. Fate had intervened and the hand had to be played out.

Jan pulled herself out of the pool, with Stephan right behind her. Dabbing herself with a large bath towel, she glanced upward toward the balcony and waved. He waved back, then left the balcony and slouched in a chair. A few minutes later she and Stephan entered the room.

"How come you didn't come to the pool like you said you would?"

"I guess I just wasn't in the mood for swimming. Maybe tomorrow, Steph."

"I was disappointed, too. I thought it would be fun, all of us together," Jan said.

"I'm sorry. I guess I'm just an old stick in the mud."

"Well, I'm going to get out of this wet suit," she said, leaving for her room.

Bob waited until Jan closed the door. "Stephan, I want a favor from you."

"What's that, Dad?"

"I'm going to take Jan out for dinner this evening. I want you to stay here in the room. You can have room service bring you anything you want to eat, and you'll have TV to watch."

"I guess you wanta go dancin', too, huh?"

"That's the idea, son. Do you mind?"

"Gosh no, Dad. I can have anything I want to eat?"

"Anything, and I promise we won't stay out late."

"Did you get her flowers?"

"Yes, I put them in her room."

When Jan entered her room, her gaze caught sight of the bouquet of roses sitting on the small table. She smiled when she read the card with its inscription of love and the invitation to dinner.

Bob, wearing a dark western suit, went to Jan's door and knocked. He looked at Jan, his heart melting at the sight of her. She looked ravishing in a dark satin green dress, which matched her eyes perfectly. "You look lovely."

"And, so do you." She kissed him, then spoke softly. "The flowers are beautiful. Thank you, kind sir," she beamed.

"Beautiful flowers for a beautiful lady," he said, taking her in his arms.

"You look so handsome tonight. I don't think I've ever seen you in a suit before." She could feel the warmth of his breath against her cheek.

"Are you ready to go?" he asked softly.

"Yes, but what about Stephan? Is he going with us?"

"No, it's just you and me tonight. It'll be a treat for him to order room service. Besides, we might do a little dancing."

She gazed into his eyes and smiled. "I love you," she said, feeling herself being drawn to him, then his lips caressed her cheek.

"The feeling is mutual," he said.

When they arrived at the Ramada Inn, the hostess greeted them, then led them to a table. The room expressed a sensual luxury. At the far end, a spacious, polished hardwood dance floor was provided, joined by a carpeted, raised platform containing musical instruments for evening entertainment.

A waiter approached the table and handed each a menu. "Would you care for anything to drink before ordering dinner?"

Jan ordered a vodka martini with extra olives and Bob ordered a screwdriver. They scanned the menu in silence while waiting for their drinks.

Bob caught sight of a lone woman taking a table near theirs; it was Patricia Duncan. Jan hadn't seen the eye contact and signal between them; her attention was taken with the menu.

Soon the waiter brought their drinks, then took their order.

Bob excused himself to call and check on Stephan. When he was out of sight, Patricia approached Jan.

"Pardon me, I couldn't help notice you sitting here. You're the woman I thought I recognized at the wine shop."

"Yes, I remember you. It's strange seeing you again..."

"It's just a coincidence. I work here. May I sit down, Miss..."

"I'm Jan, and you're?"

Once again she seemed mesmerized by Jan. "My name's Patricia Duncan. Excuse me for staring, but you look so much like the woman I knew."

"Yes...I'm sorry about her death. Did you know her well?"

"Yes. She was a publisher who owned the Dove Publishing Company in New York. She was here for only a few days attending a writer's conference." Patricia's gaze held fast to Jan's, but she saw no detectable impact in her eyes.

Jan dropped her eyes, feeling slightly self conscious under Patricia's stare. "Such a short time, but I guess if I remind you of her so much, I can understand your mistaking me for her," Jan said.

"Yes, it was a short time, but we became close in just those few days. For some reason she confided in me. She was a lonely woman, with no meaningful relationships, so she had buried herself in her work. She was too young for that, and I felt sorry for her. I'd noticed that she was rather dowdy looking, and I was able to talk her into changing her hairstyle and showed her how to use makeup to bring out her facial features. It did wonders for her. Then we went shopping for some more appealing clothes. It was like a complete transformation. I also got her to relax and have some fun. She was like a different person when she left. I'd hoped she would meet someone nice, but now she's dead."

Jan noted a deep sadness in the woman's eyes.

"I can see you had feelings for her. I'm sorry your friend is gone, and I'm sorry that I remind you of her."

"I guess we all have a look-alike somewhere," Patricia said. "I hope I haven't spoiled your evening. I was surprised to see you here, and when your friend left the table, well, I just had to talk with you."

"It was no problem, really. Actually I enjoyed talking with you. You seem like a very warm person," Jan said.

Patricia rose from the table, bade Jan goodbye, and left the room.

When Bob returned to the table, Jan was quick to speak.

"You remember that woman we saw at the farmers market? She was here. I just spoke with her."

He expressed fake surprise. "You did!" he exclaimed, looking around the room.

"She's gone now, but she works here."

"What did she have to say?"

"Nothing really. She saw me sitting here, and when you left, she came to the table. She said she just had to talk with me because I looked so much like her friend."

"Some coincidence, I mean, seeing her again."

"That's what she said."

There was no indication from Jan that her memory had been jogged in any way, and he let the matter drop. He knew he had to talk with Patricia again, to know of her impression of Jan since they had met. He changed the conversation while they dined, and, after eating, they stayed and danced the evening away.

Early the next morning Bob felt himself being rustled from sleep. "Hey, Stephan, let me sleep."

"C'mon, Dad, wake up. Let's take a swim in the pool before breakfast," Stephan pleaded.

Bob rolled over on his stomach. "Go get Jan to go swimming with you."

"Shoot, she's probably still sleeping, too. You guys didn't come home until after two this morning. Heck, I'll just go by myself."

"You be careful, hear?"

"I will," Stephan replied.

He waited until he heard the door close, then rose from the bed and put on his robe. He was anxious to talk with Patricia. He picked up his trousers and searched the pockets for the number of her motel, then dialed.

"Ramada Inn, can I help you?"

"Yes, I want to speak to Patricia Duncan."

"I'll check and see if she's in. One moment please."

After a short time a voice came on the line. "Patricia here."

"This is Bob Malloy. You talked with Jan. Was there any--?"

She interrupted before he could finish. "Nothing, absolutely no response to anything I said to her."

"I got the same impression from her."

"Mister Malloy, I'll tell you this. If your Jan isn't Melissa Cory, then she's got to be her twin. I paid close attention to her voice and her mannerisms. They're all there."

"Then you're convinced she's this...Melissa Cory?"

"I can't be one hundred percent sure, but there's one person I'm sure who could give positive identification, and that's Carl Justin, her business manager."

He remained silent, thinking of her impression of Jan. It was the most positive thing, so far. He loved Jan, and felt compelled to leave things like they were, but he knew he couldn't. He had to finish what he started, no matter the personal cost.

"Mister Malloy, are you there?"

"Yes, I'm still here. I suppose I must call this Mister Justin."

"It seems like the only logical thing to do."

"I know, but maybe he'll think I'm a crackpot...."

"That's a possibility, and your call may be very upsetting to him."

He felt his throat thicken, and words became difficult to speak. He was becoming more convinced that Jan was Melissa Cory, and the question he hadn't asked was now moot.

"Miss Duncan, was Melissa Cory a married woman?" He waited breathlessly for her answer.

"No, Mister Malloy, she wasn't."

"My God, she was right," he muttered under his breath. After a moment, he said, "Thank you, Miss Duncan."

He slowly lowered the phone to its cradle, then slumped onto the bed. Questions about his judgement were flooding his mind. Why didn't I just take her back to the ranch and have the relationship with her we both wanted? Why didn't I listen to her? Am I that self-righteous? he asked himself. But he knew it was too late to do anything about it now. Even though she was not married, and their lives were too far separated. He could not deny her a world of wealth and fame. He buried his face in the pillow while he regained his composure, then picked up the phone once again, knowing what he must do.

"Information. What city please?"

"New York, Dove Publishing Company."

"Dove Publishing Company. How may I direct your call?"

"I want to talk with a Mister Justin."

He waited nervously. The phone rang, once, twice, three times, then, "Carl Justin here."

"Mister Justin, my name is Bob Malloy. I live in Winthrop, Washington."

"Yes, what can I do for you?"

"This is very difficult, and I hardly know how to start, Mister Justin."

"Does it concern a manuscript you sent us?"

"No, it concerns Melissa Cory," Bob said, anxiety rising in his voice.

Carl was caught off guard. Why, after all these months, would someone call concerning Melissa? Still he responded calmly. "Who did you say this was, and what about Miss Cory?"

In Bob's mind there was no easy approach. He had to be blunt and up front. "I think Melissa Cory is with me and has been for several months."

There was dead silence on the line. He waited patiently, knowing what he had said was shocking news. "Hello, Mister Justin, are you there?"

Carl listened in shock to Bob's statement. Anger flared within him, thinking this was a crank call. "I don't know who you are, or what your game is, Mister--"

Bob immediately cut him off. "This is no game, believe me when I say it's more difficult for me than you. You must listen to what I have to say...it's very important, especially to you and the woman I think is Melissa Cory."

Again there was a short pause. "Okay, you got my attention, but it had better make sense."

"I know you think she's dead. I also know you had a memorial service for her, which means there was no positive identification under the circumstances of her supposed death."

"Where did you learn this information?" Carl blurted out.

"I talked with Patricia Duncan. You made contact with her on several occasions. One, checking on Melissa's whereabouts, and two, telling her of Melissa's death."

"I see," Carl muttered.

"Mister Justin, I found this woman wondering around in some pretty desolate country. I don't know how she got into her situation, but she was hurt, a head injury. She can't remember anything of her past. I brought her to Seattle, hoping she might see something familiar to jog her memory. That's when we ran into Patricia Duncan. She looked like she'd seen a ghost. I followed up on that, found out where she worked and asked her to talk with Jan...Melissa. She's pretty sure she is Melissa, and she suggested I call you."

"This is just too bizarre to be believable. Why did it take you so long to do something?"

"Mister Justin, Winthrop is a small town with a small-town marshall. He did all he could. He had AVIS and the FBI do a fingerprint check, and they came up with zilch. He also put her picture in all the major northwest papers. We had no idea she came from so far away. I kept hoping she would get her memory back. I was at a loss to know where to start, and it was just by chance that I thought Seattle may be as good as any place to start."

"Describe the woman to me," Carl said after a moment of silence.

"She's about five-foot-two, maybe a hundred twenty to twenty-five pounds. Her hair is auburn and just touches her shoulders. She's left-handed and has a small scar just at the edge of her left eyebrow.

Carl listened to the description. For the most part it fit Melissa, but thought it also could be many women, until he described the small scar. When he heard that, his stomach knotted. "Jesus," Carl uttered into the phone, then paused. "Can you bring this woman to New York?"

"I could, but Jan...or Melissa doesn't have any idea what I've been doing. Perhaps, if you showed up here in Seattle, the shock of suddenly seeing you, may have some positive effect. In any case, you could make a positive identification."

"I certainly could. I've known her since she was a little girl. Yes, I will come to Seattle, but if this is some kind of scam, you'll pay dearly."

"I assure you, all I want is an identification. She deserves that much, Mister Justin."

"I'll catch the first flight in the morning. Where shall I meet you?"

"What time will you arrive in Seattle?"

"I know there's a flight out of here at eight o'clock. With the time difference, I should be there by three o'clock your time."

"I'll have a room reserved in your name at the Red Lion Motor Inn. It's right across from the airport. I'll contact you there," Bob said, then hung up the phone.

He doffed his robe, shaved and showered. He was dressing, when Stephan came back to the room. "Get yourself showered up, son. We'll see if the lady's awake and get some breakfast."

"I thought you were goin' to sleep until noon."

"I was, but you woke me, and I couldn't get back to sleep. So get with it. We're going to a baseball game today."

The next day was spent touring the Seattle Center, then Bob suggested they go back to the Red Lion for a late lunch. He wanted to be there when Carl arrived. It was nearly three when they entered the dining room. A waitress brought them their menus and poured coffee.

"What would you like to drink, Stephan?" Bob asked.

"Can I have some coffee, like you guys?"

"I guess so, as long as you put a lot of milk in it," Bob answered, then told the waitress to pour him a cup, too.

Bob looked at the menu, his mind was not on food, but on Carl Justin. He looked at his watch; it was a few minutes past three. It would take Carl at least half an hour to get his baggage and catch the airporter to the motel.

"Did you like the Seattle Center, Steph?" Bob asked, trying to hide the apprehension building in him. He didn't want Jan to sense anything, and, so far, he'd been pretty good at concealing all that he'd been doing.

"Yeah, but we coulda' stayed there and got somethin' to eat."

"I think you've had enough junk food," Jan said.

"The rides sure were fun. I wish we had rides like that at home."

"I know. We spent a lot of time at the center just so you could get your fill of rides, but everything comes to an end, sometime," Bob said, then shot a quick glance at Jan, though she didn't see it.

The waitress returned to take their orders, but Jan had not decided what she would have. The waitress left, saying she would return in a few minutes.

Ten minutes passed, and Bob looked at his watch once more; it was now three-twenty. He had to think of some excuse to leave Jan and get to Carl's room. The waitress returned to take their orders. After the waitress left with their orders, Bob pulled his wallet out and looked inside.

"I don't have enough money with me. I guess we spent too much at the center. I'll have to run up to the room and get some checks," he said, asking Stephan to go with him. "We won't be gone long, Jan."

Jan smiled with pride when she watched the two of them walk away.

Out of sight of the dining room, Bob stopped at the desk and inquired if a Carl Justin had registered.

"Let me check," the clerk said, studying the computer. "Yes, he's in Room 110. It's right down that corridor, sir. Would you like me to call him on the phone?"

"No, he's expecting me. Thank you," Bob replied.

Stephan was in a state of confusion. "Who's expectin' you, Dad? And who's Carl Justin? I thought we were goin' to the room."

"You'll find out what's going on in a minute, son."

He knocked on the door to Room 110, and there was an immediate response. "Mister Malloy?" The man standing in the doorway asked.

"Yes... Mister Justin?" Bob returned. He saw that the man was elderly, probably in his mid-sixties. His close-cut, wavy grey hair clung neatly at his temples, and his brown eyes sparkled through the black-rimmed glasses garnishing his face. His charcoal-gray suit was tailor made, and Bob knew he was from a world he had never seen.

Carl Justin stepped aside and let them enter the room. "Is Melissa with you?" he asked anxiously.

"Yes. She's in the dining room."

Stephan was still mystified to what was happening, even though he grasped who they were talking about, he'd never heard the name Melissa. "Dad...what's goin' on?"

Bob stood looking down at his son. After a long moment's pause, he said, "This is Mister Carl Justin. It's possible that we may learn who Jan really is."

"Does he know Jan? How would he know her? I ain't never seen him before."

Bob looked at Carl, then Stephan. "Mister Justin is from New York. He's going to talk with Jan. Her real name may be Melissa Cory, and that's what he's going to tell us."

Still confused, Stephan paused, then asked, "If Jan is this Melissa, will he take her away?"

"I suppose he will, to help her get her memory back."

"Are we goin' with her, Dad?" Stephan asked, his eyes darting between his father and Carl.

"No, Stephan. She'll be going back with Mister Justin alone."

"Mister Malloy, with all due respect, I think we should go and see her," Carl suggested impatiently.

"Please, Mister Justin, I haven't told Stephan or Jan that I have had contact with you. Neither of them knew I was meeting you here today. Let me at least explain to my son."

"Yes, of course...I'm sorry." Carl stepped aside to give them some privacy.

Bob placed his arm around Stephan's shoulder. He felt this was the hardest thing he ever had to tell his son aside from having to tell him about his mother's death.

"I want you to try and understand, son. If Jan is Melissa, then she is a very important person. She owns a very large publishing company. A lot of people depend upon her. We helped her all that we could, but now, she must get more help to regain her memory and return to the life she had before."

There was a tremor in Stephan's voice, and his eyes started to fill with moisture. "But, Dad, you love her and she loves you. She told me she did. And I don't want her to go back now...I love her, too. She belongs with us."

Bob could see the tears in Stephan's eyes, and his voice cracked with emotion. "I know, I know, son. You're right, I do love her, and we've been through a lot in a short time, but if she is truly Melissa Cory, she must go with Mister Justin, and we must accept it."

Stephan's shoulders slumped when he tried to comprehend what his father was telling him. "Will she come to visit us when she gets her memory back? Can we go see her?"

Carl, hearing the anxiety in the boy's voice, came to their side. "I can see, this is very difficult for both of you. If this woman is Melissa, I'm sure you would be welcome anytime," he assured.

"There, you see. Now I think Mister Justin has waited long enough. He's anxious to see her, too," Bob said.

"Yes, shall we go?" Carl urged, walking toward the door.

"I think it would be better if you talked with her alone. We'll wait in the lobby to see what happens."

"As you wish, Mister Malloy. Assuming she is...I suppose you'll want to say goodbye to her," Carl said.

"I think it would be better for both of us if we didn't see each other."

"Mister Malloy, I've known Melissa all her life. The boy says that she's in love with you. If that's true, then it's the first time in her life she has loved anyone. I'm afraid she never had much luck in that department. Mostly, I think, because of her wealth and intellect. Because of that, she had become a very bitter and cynical woman. Please don't hurt her by just leaving and saying nothing to her."

Bob flashed Carl a startled look. He found it hard to believe that the woman Carl Justin just described was the same woman he'd known and lived with for the past nine months. Jan was anything but cynical and bitter. She was a person full of enthusiasm and love.

"Mister Justin," Bob offered, "if the woman you came for is Melissa Cory, all that has happened between the two of us has happened between Jan and myself. When you get her home and the help she needs to regain her memory, and once she realizes who she is and what her responsibilities are, she will accept that."

"You know you could change your lifestyle."

Bob's forehead wrinkled in thought for a moment. "That's true, I could. But it wouldn't work. Oh, maybe we'd be happy for a while but I'm afraid that concrete jungle would destroy both of us, in time. No, Mister Justin, we're from two different worlds. It would never work."

"As you wish, Mister Malloy. Shall I tell her anything for you?"

"Tell her anything you wish. Now you had better get down to the dining room. She'll be wondering what happened to us."

Carl Justin walked into the dining room and scanned the area. He was remembering Melissa as she had appeared for so many years. At first his eyes passed over her when he viewed the room. But she was the only woman sitting at a table by herself. The fact the food had been placed at two vacant settings further convinced him she was the woman he was seeking. The transformation astounded him. Could this be the Melissa he had known? The woman was beautiful and radiant. He could not help staring at her. Little by little he picked up on features that could not be hidden; it **was** really her. He quickly approached the table.

"Jan?" He asked with a broad smile.

She looked up, surprised at seeing the elderly gentleman.

"Yes," she replied, returning his smile.

"May I sit down, please?"

She was surprised that this man knew her name and wished to sit with her. She gazed at his warm face. It seemed familiar to her, but she couldn't place it. Yet, she felt drawn to him.

"Well, I'm expecting the people I came with. I don't know what's taking them so long, but you can join me until they return."

"Thank you," he said, pulling the chair back to sit down. "You don't remember me, do you?"

Jan studied him while trying to deter the strange feelings she was beginning to have. "Have we met before?"

"Yes, we have," Carl replied.

"Your voice is vaguely familiar...where did we meet?"

"Does the name Melissa Cory mean anything to you?" he asked, ignoring her question.

She straightened in her chair. Who was this man asking these questions of her, and where were Bob and Stephan? Her mouth suddenly felt dry. She wet her lips with her tongue while she glanced quickly around the room. The name he mentioned echoed through her mind, repeating itself over and over, like it would never stop; it, too, had a familiar sound.

She felt a sudden strangeness surround her. She was becoming nervous. Her legs became weak, even though she was sitting. Her eyes shot around the room again in search of Bob and Stephan. She was suddenly becoming warm, despite the air-conditioned room. Her gaze rested steadily on Carl Justin. "Who are you?"

Carl could see she was becoming overwrought. He'd seen her like this before, and it sent him back in time.

At the early age of three, she was reading material beyond her age group. Her parents, seeing her aptitude, worked diligently with her. When she grew older, her insatiable desire for books also grew. Her mother had died in an auto accident when she was twelve. Shortly thereafter, her father gently led her into the publishing business, never pushing her, but giving her the ground training from the bottom up, and she had accepted it willingly.

When she had reached the age of twenty-one, her father died of a sudden heart attack. Consequently, she had inherited the Dove Romance Publishing Corporation. It wasn't that she had been thrown into the business with his passing, but, in fact, had grown up with it. She had revolved around the publishing business, hence filling her life with stress. He could see the same tensions building again, but for much different reasons.

"A friend, a very good friend, dear. I'm Carl Justin, and you're Melissa Cory. Try to think back in time. I've known you since you were a baby," he said.

She listened to his voice, and suddenly her eyes opened wide, as it became more familiar. His voice echoed through the canyons of her mind, filling vacant caves with images of her forgotten past, unmasking that hidden portion of her memory. She stared at him, her mind flooded with images of who and what she was.

"Carl!!" she exclaimed. She stood up, leaned across the table and threw her arms around him. Tears flowed from her eyes, and he felt her trembling, sobbing body when he held her.

Bob and Stephan remained in the lobby at a vantage point where she could not see them. After seeing her eventual reaction to Carl, Bob knew that she had recognized him. He saw her hands clasped upon Carl's when they sat back down. She was talking rapidly and smiling, and Carl was listening attentively.

An emptiness ravaged his soul. Stephan stood silently at his side, his eyes flitting between Jan and his father. He saw the tears in his father's eyes.

Bob watched Jan's reaction to Carl, his good sense told him everything they had shared was fading. He couldn't hold her to the feelings that existed between them. She had found her former life once again.

"Come on, Stephan. I think it's time we go."

"But, Dad, you just can't walk away from her. It isn't fair," Stephan said sadly.

"Life isn't always fair. It's something you'll learn as you get older. It's better this way. I know it's hard for you to understand, but she's not Jan any more. She's Melissa Cory. Just look at her. She has her memory back and she seems very happy. She'll be going back to New York with Mister Justin and resume her life."

Stephan looked up at him. "But she told me she loved you, and she saved my life. She made me understand things. She was good to us, Dad. I don't want her to go."

"She has to, Stephan. It just can't be any other way."

"You knew this was going to happen, didn't you?" he asked solemnly.

"I knew that some day something would happen. I didn't figure it would happen this way, but it did and we can't change it," Bob said, putting his western hat on and pulling it down over his eyes so Stephan would not see the tears collecting in them. Then added, "Come on, son, let's get our stuff packed up and get out of here."

Once their belongings were packed and the bill paid, they left the motel. Walkin across the parking lot to the pickup, Stephan asked, "Do you think she'll remember us?"

"I'm sure she will...for a while, just like we'll remember her."

"I'll never forget her," Stephan said firmly.

"I have a feeling neither of us ever will, son," he replied, drawing him close.

SEVENTEEN

Through her excitement of the moment, Melissa suddenly realized that Bob and Stephan had not returned. She started to wonder what was going on.

"Carl, how is it that you're here in Seattle?"

"I know it must be confusing to you, since Mister Malloy didn't tell you what he was doing. He brought you to Seattle in the hope you might recognize something that would spur your memory. It's not important how, but Patricia Duncan more or less confirmed your identity, then he called me yesterday and asked if I would come and make a more positive identification."

Melissa had completely forgotten Patricia. Now her memory flashed back to the wine shop. Bob must have found out where she worked and talked with her. Yes, he set it up for her to talk with me. It wasn't just a coincidence at all, she thought to herself.

"Have you talked to him today?"

"Yes, he came to my room. It was apparent to me that he was sure you were Melissa Cory, but I think he was secretly hoping you weren't. He and his son have been watching us from the lobby. Perhaps he's still there."

"Wait here, Carl," she said anxiously. She ran into the lobby, her eyes searching for them. She approached the desk.

"Could you ring Mister Malloy's room, please?"

"Mister Malloy? I'm afraid he's checked out, Miss."

"How...when...he couldn't have," she insisted. She couldn't believe he would leave without an explanation or even a word of goodbye.

"I'm afraid he has, about twenty minutes ago, Miss."

"Oh... thank you," she said softly, then slowly walked back into the dining room and Carl.

She stared straight ahead while tears were filling her eyes. "He's gone...he left without a word."

There was a moment of silence, and Carl saw the effect on her. "He thought it would be better this way. I wanted him to talk to you, but he wouldn't. He must have seen your reaction to me and assumed your memory returned."

"All the more reason he should have stayed. He doesn't care about me."

"I believe he cares a great deal about you, and so does the boy."

"Poor Stephan. He sure was a struggle. It took me along time, but at least I won his love and respect," she said.

She remembered her former relationships. So many men were only interested in her money, but, the few who weren't, always seemed to run from her because they were intimidated by her intellect. With the amnesia, the barriers with which she had shielded herself were gone, and she fell hopelessly in love with Bob Malloy.

Numbed, she leaned back in her chair. She could understand Bob's prideful feelings, but to leave without so much as a goodbye, disappointed and angered her deeply.

Her lips quivered when she spoke. "What's the matter with me, Carl? Why is it always the same? I was loved as Jan, but, as Melissa Cory, they run from me."

"He didn't run from you, but rather what you represent. It's obvious the man's in love with you, but he feels that you're worlds apart from each other," Carl said.

Melissa suddenly felt alone, and the past nine months had not really happened. With everything they had shared and felt for each other, she could not believe Bob could just walk out. 'I guess I didn't know him as well as I thought I did', she told herself. "You say it's obvious that he loves me. Do you really, in your heart, believe that?"

"Yes, I do. Very much so, dear."

"Well," she said, taking a deep breath, "to use an old cliche, `it is better to have loved and lost than not to have loved at all'."

"It'll take a little time, my dear, but the scars of a lost love heal with time," Carl said, patting her hand.

Melissa straightened in her chair and held her head high. "Of course, you're right. I need to get back to work." She was trying to steal herself from the hurt, disappointment, and anger she felt, thinking if she threw herself into her work, she could forget the past nine months. "I want to leave on the next flight out of this city and out of this state."

Her curt words triggered Carl's memory to the past. He had seen the defensive screen she had placed around herself for several years. It, in fact, had accounted for most of the stress he had seen building within her. Now, he saw the same pattern developing once again, pulling herself back into a shell. He knew she had been miserably lonely, yet longed for someone who could accept her for herself, not for her wealth.

Carl sat silently seeing the determination in her. At this moment he knew there was nothing he could say to make her reconsider her decision to leave for New York.

While looking at her, his expression changed; he couldn't believe the difference in her physical appearance. She was absolutely striking. Her hair, her makeup, everything was different. She had always worn her beautiful auburn hair in a bun, and her face had been masked by heavy, red, horned-rimmed glasses that were not at all attractive. She wore no cosmetics at all and constantly wore dresses and business suits that would have looked more natural on an older woman. Now she sat before him dressed in western attire. It was quite a change.

Melissa saw the puzzled expression on Carl's face. "You have something on your mind. What is it?"

"Yes, I want to know what happened to you. How did the amnesia thing happen?"

Her mind traveled back to her arrival in Seattle, the writer's conference, and the way Patricia Duncan had helped her personally.

"It's a long story, Carl. Are you sure you want to hear it?"

"Definitely. It has all the marks of a good story," he said.

Carl listened patiently. She reminded him of the itinerary for the conferences in Seattle and Spokane. Her voice seemed unapparent to her, for she was reliving that portion of her life in her mind.

She had traveled the United States many times, but always by air, missing its beauty. She had read of the High Cascade Highway in a travel brochure. Procuring a map of Washington, she sought out the route through the Cascade Mountains to Spokane. She became fascinated by the thought of making that drive from Seattle.

"When I arrived in Seattle for the conference, I got acquainted with Patricia Duncan. For some reason we took to each other, and she is responsible for my change in appearance."

"I must say, it's quite an improvement," Carl said.

"It took a little getting used to, but it sure helped my self-esteem."

"Perhaps, with this new image, things will change for the better at home."

The words `at home' struck at her heart, and her eyes started to fill with tears, remembering that her home had been at the ranch with a man she loved. She was still vulnerable to her feelings, though she tried to appear otherwise. Using a napkin, she wiped at her tears. She looked at Carl and she saw the pity for her in his eyes.

There was a moment of silence between them, then Carl spoke. "What happened when you left Seattle? Mister Malloy told me he found you wandering around in the hills."

"Yes, he did. Had he not found me, I most likely would be dead."

"Everyone thought you were. I mean, killed in an auto accident. But, we couldn't understand what you were doing in Idaho."

" An accident!" she exclaimed "I stopped at a motel in Winthrop, but there wasn't a room to be had. It was at night, and I hadn't locked the car. When I got back on the road, this man and woman popped up in the backseat. They made me stop and get in the back while the woman drove. They took all my money, traveler's checks and identification, and then the man literally threw me out of the car. I remember falling over the edge of the road and down into a ravine. I was unconscious and when I came to, I walked until I couldn't walk anymore. That's when Bob found me. It had to have been the man and woman who were killed in my car."

"There was no mention of a man in the accident. There wasn't much left of the car or the body they found. They did find the serial number on the engine, and we just assumed it was you who had died in that accident."

Melissa sighed deeply. "I don't know if I'm fortunate or not. Bob's run away from me." She paused a moment. "Perhaps it's for the best. What time is the next flight to New York?"

He looked at his watch. "Well, it's five-thirty now, and there's a non-stop flight leaving at ten tonight."

"Good. Let's take it," she replied. "I'll pack my things, freshen up, and meet you in the bar."

"Melissa, maybe you shouldn't be too hasty. I mean, maybe you should take some time and try contacting Mister Malloy, talk to him. It's obvious to me that you're both in love. If you leave as he did, I suspect you'll both be miserable."

Melissa stared coldly at Carl. "He didn't have to leave the way he did. We could have talked. Obviously he didn't care enough."

"If you would have seen him and the boy as I did--"

Melissa interrupted him. "I don't want to talk about it, Carl, it's done."

"As you wish, my dear," he replied.

She packed her few belongings, then, disrobing and wrapping a towel around her hair, she climbed into the shower. She let the warm water spray over her body, then closed her eyes while she held her face to the spray. Visions of Bob appeared in her mind. Despite the bitterness building inside, her heart ached for him, and she could hear the tender words of love he had spoken to her.

It suddenly became clear to her that the reason he left was not only because their lives were worlds apart, but because he wanted her to return to the life to which he thought she was dedicated and probably would be most happy. This was his way of expressing his love for her. But what he didn't know was that she was not happy with her life in New York City. Had he only spoken to her before he left so abruptly, she could have explained.

Was her position more important than the happiness she had found with this man? She found herself involuntarily answering these questions loudly. "No! No!"

She climbed out of the shower with a renewed vigor. Mister Malloy might be running from her, but she was not running from him. She quickly dressed, applied her makeup, then ran a brush through her hair. After throwing the remaining items into the suitcase, she grabbed her purse and left the room.

She walked briskly into the bar and spotted Carl sitting in a booth. He smiled when she came toward him.

"Carl, I have something to tell you."

He was about to stand up. "Sit down, Carl!" Melissa ordered. "You may not like what I have to say."

Carl slid back into his seat, and she sat across from him. "I'm not going back with you, Carl."

Carl listened to her and wondered what could have happened in such a short time to change her mind. "Not going, but you have to. What about the business? You have responsibilities."

"The company has gotten along without me for nine months--"

He interrupted her, "Do you have any idea what we were going through without you? We need--"

There was a firmness in Melissa's voice. "No, Carl, you don't need me. But I **do** know where I'm needed, and it's not stuck in an office making decisions that any number of other people could make. I'm going back to where I found a man who loves me for myself, and whom I love. You said yourself that I shouldn't be too hasty."

Carl looked at her with a half smile. "You're not serious, Melissa."

Melissa stood her ground with him. "I've never been more serious about anything in my life. It's time I started living for **me** instead of living for a business. Negotiate the best deal you can for a sale, Carl."

"Sell the company! I would give that some serious consideration, dear. For instance, suppose the situation between you and this man doesn't work out the way you want it to?"

"I'll cross that bridge if I come to it, Carl. The amnesia came unexpectedly, but it was the best thing that could have happened to me. In these past months, I've been happier than all the years I'd forgotten. Bob and Stephan need me, and I need them. What my life had been in the past, is just that, **past**. I'm not going to sacrifice my best chance at happiness."

"Who knows better than I, except for yourself. Maybe you have a point," Carl said. "I did talk to him about living in New York where the two of you would be together, but he said that would probably destroy your relationship."

"He wouldn't be happy in New York. He's a westerner through and through."

"The same goes for you. Will you be happy living away from the city?"

"Oh, yes. I've experienced life away from that stress-filled concrete jungle. And, to tell you the truth, I **love** it. But, more important, I love Bob, and I want to spend the rest of my life with him and his son. Carl, don't try to talk me out of something I haven't had for some time, a family."

Carl could see the determination reflected in her face, and he wanted her to be happy. "Well, I guess you've made your mind up," he said. "Is there some way to get in touch with him before he gets to his ranch?"

"No, I want to be home when they arrive. I'm going to hire a limousine to take me there, but I'll need some money. How much have you got on you?"

"About five hundred," he replied, reaching for his wallet.

"Good. Four hundred should do me."

When she said the word 'home', a warmth filled her body. She thought of Bob's dreams. She wanted to be a part of that and share in the rewards of making the ranch a success. She was determined to make Bob realize that her business, the prestige, and the money meant as little to her as it did to him.

After making the arrangements for the limousine, they waited in the lobby for it to arrive.

"What am I going to tell the people back home?"

"Tell them the truth. That I've lost my head and that I'm in love with a **wonderful** man!"

When the limousine pulled up to the entrance, Carl handed Melissa's suitcase to the driver.

"You are absolutely sure about selling the firm?"

"Yes, but put a condition on the sale. I want the people with the firm guaranteed continued employment for at least one year."

"That will probably stall a quick sale," he replied.

"Maybe, but that's what I want. They're all good people. Besides, there's no rush. You have my address and phone number, so just keep me posted."

"Okay, my dear. If anyone would have told me that, when you left for the seminar, the events you have explained to me were going to happen, I never would have believed them. You're a changed woman, Melissa, not only in your appearance but in your heart."

"I have only Bob to thank for that," she said, flashing a big smile.

"Melissa, I wish you happiness and love for the rest of your life," Carl said, squeezing her hand tenderly. "I'll miss you terribly. You've become like a daughter to me."

Melissa hugged him and gave him a kiss on the cheek. "Thank you, Carl. I know I'm doing the right thing. For me, the time for love is **now**, so I'd better take it; for it may never come again. Will you come to my wedding?" she asked, thinking positively.

"You couldn't keep me away," he replied, his eyes twinkling.

"I'll let you know when. Goodbye, and take care of yourself."

"Goodbye," he said, giving her one last hug. He watched the limousine pull away from the entrance and finally out of sight.

The driver headed toward the freeway. Melissa settled back in the seat and stretched her legs. It was going to be a long ride to the ranch, she thought. Then a sudden urgency filled her and sparked an idea. The entrance to Interstate-5 was just ahead. She tapped the driver on the shoulder. "I've changed my mind. Take me to Yakima."

"Yes, ma'am. You're the boss," he replied, bypassing the exit and heading east.

"How fast will this thing go?" she asked.

"Faster than I like to drive," he responded.

She calculated the time it took to drive the pickup from Yakima to the Red Lion Motor Inn. Her best guess was that Bob and Stephan had left between four and four-thirty. That would put them in Yakima between seven and seven-thirty. She looked at her watch; it was five minutes after six.

"Get me to Yakima no later then nine o'clock and you've earned a hundred-dollar bonus," she said.

"Plus possible speeding tickets?" he returned.

"You got it," she replied with a chuckle.

"Well, let's see what this thing will do," he said.

Two and half hours later they topped the crest of the last hill leading into Yakima. The evening sun flashed brightly off of the windows of the city's buildings when they wound their way down the mountainside to the valley.

They were on the flat now and approaching the city limits. Melissa crossed her fingers, closed her eyes, and said a small prayer that Bob had not yet left Yakima for the ranch.

"Take me to Yakima Meadows. Do you know how to get there?" she asked.

"Yes. I've been there several times," he replied.

"Good. I've only been there once, and I'm not sure just how to get there myself."

The gate was open and she noticed several horse trailers parked in an area about a hundred yards away. People were milling about. Some were unloading horses and entering a large building.

She directed the driver to proceed to the livestock barns. When they reached the area where they had kept Blue, she told the driver to stop. She got out of the car and walked along the stalls. When she reached Blue's stall, she looked in. Blue was standing with his head in the feeder. He pulled his head up, sensing her presence, then looked in her direction and nickered. Opening the stall door, she walked up to Blue and gave him a pat on the neck. Once again he nickered, then dipped his head into the feeder to get another mouthful of grain.

"I see someone has already fed you. Darn, if it was Bob, he probably won't be back again tonight. I wish you could talk Blue. Maybe you could tell me what I need to know," she said, then gave him another pat on the rump and left the stall.

She stopped at the office building. The light was still on. An elderly man was sitting at a desk reading a newspaper. He looked up as she entered. "Can I help you, young lady?"

"Would you happen to know a man by the name of Bob Malloy?" she asked.

"Can't say that I do right off. Is he supposed to meet you here?"

"No...not exactly. I just came to see if he had picked up his horse, but he's still in his stall."

"There was a fella' in here a little while ago wanting to know if he could pick his horse up in the morning."

"That must have been him. Did he tell you where he was staying?"

"No, ma'am. But I told him he'd have to pick his horse up tonight, because there won't be anybody here tomorrow. Told him I'd be here till about eleven-thirty, or as soon as those local cowboys clear out."

"Did he have a young boy with him?"

"As a matter of fact, he did."

"That's the man I'm looking for," she replied with a smile.

"You can wait here in the office for him."

"Thank you, but that won't be necessary. I'll wait for him outside."

She had the driver take her back to the stall area. She paid his fee, then, she gave him the hundred-dollar tip, and watched when the limousine pulled away.

The night was turning dusk and the evening was sultry. She looked at her watch; it was nine-forty. They should be coming soon, she thought. She looked down along the stall buildings and listened for the sound of his truck.

It was her intention to surprise Bob and Stephan, but it had gotten dark enough that the photoelectric lamps, stationed throughout the ground, started to lighten the area. A row of them was situated between the buildings containing the stalls. They flooded the area with light, leaving no shadow in which to hide. She entered the empty stall next to Blue and patiently waited.

A half an hour had passed when she heard the faint sound of a motor. Looking out of the stall door, she saw the light of an approaching vehicle. It stopped for a moment, then turned in between the two buildings and came toward her. She ducked back into the stall. Her heart was pounding with excitement and apprehension. What if, after all this, Bob isn't happy to see me? she asked herself.

The vehicle stopped. She heard the doors open and Bob and Stephan talking when they lowered the gate of the horse trailer. Then she heard the sound of the door latch to Blue's stall. Bob turned on the stall light and was telling Stephan to gather up the tack that hung on the wall.

She stepped out of the stall she had been hiding in and stood in the doorway of Blue's. Bob was putting a halter on the horse and had his back to her. Stephan was busy taking the tack off the wall. He turned toward the door, his arms loaded. His eyes opened wide at seeing her standing there. He suddenly dropped the tack and shouted, "Jan!...I mean, Melissa!" He ran to her and hugged her tightly.

Bob turned instantly at Stephan's sudden outburst and saw Stephan with his arms around her. Melissa had one arm around Stephan, but her eyes were locked on Bob. He stood facing her for a moment. Neither spoke, and they became oblivious to everything around them while their eyes held to each other. The lead strap dropped from his hand, and in one step Bob gathered Melissa in his arms. Their lips met hungrily in a long, passionate kiss.

The three of them stood there, silently holding onto one another, the sudden impact of her presence leaving no room for words.

Her eyes filled with tears of joy, and they clung to each other. "Why did you leave me? What would make you do such a foolish thing?"

"You're an important and very rich person, Jan. When I saw your reaction to Carl Justin, I knew your memory had returned. I just thought it better to make a clean break. You would go back to the world you knew, and I would go to mine and savor a wonderful memory. Do you really remember everything now?"

"Yes...I do remember everything. I remember how drab my life was. Sure, I had money, but nothing else. I was miserably lonely, Bob. There was no meaning to my life until I met you. You had no idea who I was, but you fell in love with me for myself, and **that**, my darling, is what's important. I've been searching for the kind of love you have given me all my life, and now my journey is over.

"I do love you, Jan, but you have responsibilities and people depending upon you. I don't think I could adjust to your lifestyle and all those high-faultin' people you know.

"You won't have to, Bob. I love the ranch and the horses."

"But what about your publishing company?" he asked.

"I told Carl to sell it. I have what I want right here with the two of you...if you'll have me."

Bob looked deeply into her eyes. "Are you sure?"

"Yes, Bob, I am."

He stood back for a moment, then looked at Stephan who was still holding onto her. "What do you think, son? Should we take her back to the ranch with us?" He was beaming from ear to ear.

"Yeah, you better take her back to the ranch, Dad, 'cause if you don't, I'm goin' with her," he said, hugging her tighter.

Bob embraced Melissa, and once more their lips met in a desire that was still to be fulfilled. He drew back from her, their eyes staring deeply into each other's, and they both saw the embers of passion that had been smoldering for too long.

"Come on, you two," he said, "let's go home. We have a lot of plans to make for our future."

About the Author

I retired in 1995 from the government. Prior to this I started thinking about what I could do after my retirement. In 1988 I started to write: a crime story, a paranormal story, and a science fiction story and in the confusion, several short stories. I may add; these have never been published.

My wife and I built our home, and we have lived there twenty-six years. We like to fish and go camping. When we are not camping or fishing, I am at my computer writing.